A Friend Indeed

"Bernard," said Maya, "did you hear what Snooky just told me?"

"What is it?"

"The hostess of the party he went to last night—well, she died. They say she was *poisoned*."

Bernard looked up from his desk. "You're kidding."

"No."

"That's horrible." Bernard felt strangely offended. Murders, he felt, should not happen in Ridgewood, Connecticut.

"Well, he's pretty upset."

"Mmmm-hmmm. Do you think he did it?"

"Bernard, please. It's not like he *knew* any of those people, really. He just met them last night. I mean, Snooky is always getting into some kind of trouble, but he never actually ran afoul of the law before."

"Sweetheart, your brother did not murder his hostess. The police must know that. All the same—"

"What?"

"All the same, I wonder who did," said Bernard.

Bantam Crime Line Books offers the finest in classic and modern American murder mysteries. Ask your bookseller for the books you have missed.

GLORIA DANK

FRIENDS
TILL THE END

BANTAM BOOKS
NEW YORK · TORONTO · LONDON · SYDNEY · AUCKLAND

FRIENDS TILL THE END

A Bantam Book / October 1989

ISBN 0-553-28152-6

Published simultaneously in the United States and Canada

Bantam Books are published by Bantam Books, a division of Bantam Doubleday Dell Publishing Group, Inc. Its trademark, consisting of the words "Bantam Books" and the portrayal of a rooster, is Registered in U.S. Patent and Trademark Office and in other countries. Marca Registrada. Bantam Books, 666 Fifth Avenue, New York, New York 10103.

PRINTED IN THE UNITED STATES OF AMERICA

KRI 0 9 8 7 6 5 4 3 2 1

TO LEIF

Cast of Characters

THE FAMILY

Laura Sloane—Walter Sloane's wife and stepmother to his two children—the party she gave was to be her last, but other than that it was, like all her parties, a great success. . . .

Walter Sloane—a thorough curmudgeon, made wealthy by his wife's death, he was hated by nearly all his friends—and his family. . . .

Isabel Sloane—Walter Sloane's beautiful daughter from his first marriage, who chose to stay at home and cook and clean for everyone. . . .

Richard Sloane—Walter Sloane's son from his first marriage—spoiled and sulky, he fought often and violently with his father. . . .

THE FRIENDS

Sam Abrams—Walter Sloane's business partner, who enjoyed taking over while Walter was away. . . .

Ruth Abrams—Sam's dithery, slow-witted wife. . . .

Harry Crandall—emeritus professor of biology and an expert on slime molds, he could paralyze an entire room of people just by talking. . . .

Heather Crandall—Harry's wife, she was obsessed by health—her own and everyone else's. . . .

Freda Simms—an eccentric widow who was jealous of the people she loved. . . .

THE OTHERS

Snooky Randolph—a wealthy young man with no particular occupation and a fantastic gift for crossword puzzles. . . .

Maya Woodruff—Snooky's older sister, who strongly disapproved of his choice of girlfriends. . . .

Bernard Woodruff—writer of children's books and armchair detective, he trusted no one except his wife Maya—and himself. . . .

Detective Jim Voelker—his habitually melancholy expression deepened as one murder inevitably followed another. . . .

1

It was a lovely party. Everyone said so; even Harry Crandall, emeritus professor of biology, who ordinarily spent
the whole evening talking about his beloved slime molds.
This evening he had been cajoled into discussing the Late
Beethoven Quartets, quite a departure for him. He was an
authority on the subject, as everyone expected he would
be. He only held forth on subjects on which he was an
authority. The host, Walter Sloane, and his wife Laura
circulated among their guests. It was a small party: just
the Sloane family and a few friends. There was only one
stranger present, a young man with a very odd name,
something like Snoopy or Ucky. Walter Sloane's daughter
had brought him along as her date. He was not one of the
usual crowd so everyone ignored him; by far the easiest way.

It was a lovely, lovely party; everyone said so. It would
have been just about perfect if the hostess had not died.
As it was, everyone enjoyed themselves very much.

"Naked masses of protoplasm," Harry Crandall was
saying, diverted momentarily by a question concerning his
favorite subject. "That's all they are. Fascinating crea-
tures, I tell you. Slime molds belong to a class of extremely peculiar organisms, *Myxomycetes* . . ."

Freda Simms gave her distinctive loud cackle. "He's
off again. Good old Harry."

Ruth Abrams looked worried. She always looked worried. She was a short heavy-set woman with the mild-mannered face of a not very intelligent sheep. "Freda," she said reproachfully. "He'll hear you."

Freda Simms smiled. Her hair tonight was red; a distinctive shade of brilliant red. It looked as if it had been painted on her head by an industrious child with finger paints. It stuck out wildly in all directions and bobbed as she talked. She spoke constantly, nervously, gesturing with a cigarette.

"I've convinced Eddie to show me how he does his makeup," she said.

Ruth Abrams looked doubtfully at Freda's boyfriend.

"Clown makeup is an art form," Freda continued. "Isn't it, Eddie?"

Eddie seemed to agree. Eddie was a silent creature; a man of few words, thought Ruth. She glanced around nervously and hoped someone would rescue her soon. Freda was a dear friend, but honestly, a *clown* . . .

Although perhaps a clown was better than Freda's last boyfriend, who had been introduced at a party much like this one. His name had been Charlie and he had been a professional skydiver. The romance had blossomed until one day Charlie had had a minor technical difficulty with his parachute.

Harry Crandall was back on the Late Beethoven Quartets again. Ruth could hear his voice droning on. Usually the host, Walter Sloane, found some minor point that he could disagree with and picked a fight—more than one party had been broken up by the women because Harry and Walter were at each other's throats over the prospects of the local baseball team, or the merit of some obscure work of literature, or that forbidden topic, politics. But tonight Harry was droning on undisturbed. That probably meant that Walter Sloane didn't know a thing about the Late Beethoven Quartets.

Ruth looked over at Walter. Tonight he seemed to be having a decent time, although the sight of his closest friends eating his food and drinking his liquor usually made him apoplectic. Rich as he was, he saved every

dime. She had been with him once in a restaurant when he called the manager over because he had put a quarter in the jukebox, which then refused to play his selection. "I want 'Old Man River,'" he had roared, to the delight of the other patrons.

Freda Simms and her boyfriend were now hotly debating something to do with the circus—Indian versus African elephants, it sounded like. Ruth cast an agonized glance around the room. Her eyes rested briefly on Isabel, Walter Sloane's daughter. She looked beautiful as always, with her straight silk-blonde hair drawn back in a knot and those striking blue eyes. She was sitting in the corner, deep in conversation with the young man she had brought along tonight. Next to them sat her teenage brother, Richard—another product of Walter Sloane's first marriage. Ruth wondered vaguely what Richard was doing here. He didn't usually put in an appearance at his parents' parties. Isabel was always there, of course, an unobtrusive presence at your elbow, offering food and drinks, scuttling back and forth from the kitchen—as though they couldn't afford to hire help, and as much as they wanted!—another example of Walter's notorious miserliness. She dragged her attention back to Freda, who had gone on to another topic and was now saying,

"The last time I was in Monte Carlo—"

Monte Carlo, indeed! Ruth felt a prickle of resentment. *Some people* didn't have the money to travel to Monte Carlo whenever they liked. Of course Freda had always been rich. She didn't know what it was like not to be. And of course she had never had children. Children made a big difference; yes, a very big difference.

Over in the corner, Isabel Sloane was saying,

"What are you doing here, Richard?"

Her brother shrugged.

"No date for tonight?" she asked teasingly. Her brother's blond good looks were very much appreciated by the female members of his high school class.

Her brother grinned at her. His usually morose face lit up.

("When he smiles he looks almost human," she had told a friend recently. "The trouble is, he never smiles.")

"Oh, shut up," Richard Sloane said, but his tone was friendly.

The young man who was with Isabel leaned back, regarding them with an amused eye.

"When I was Richard's age I couldn't stop going to parties," he said. "It was sort of a mania with me. When my brother and sister wanted to find out where I was, all they had to do was call around the neighborhood and see who was having a party. I was never invited, but I went anyway. I would do all kinds of affairs: weddings, cocktail parties, receptions. Funerals. I once got thrown out of an embassy on East Seventy-first Street in New York for crashing an official reception. The Vice-President was going to be there and they were all excited about the security breach, but all I wanted was a snack."

"I hate parties," Richard Sloane said firmly.

"Oh, well, you never know. Maybe you'll grow into it."

"Mrs. Abrams needs a drink," said Isabel and bolted

toward the bar. Her companion watched her go with a faintly worried look in his eyes. But all he said was:

"Know anything about Boccherini?"

"No," said Richard.

"Well, this is your big chance. There's someone over there who appears to be an expert."

Harry Crandall had switched topics once again and was now being dazzling and authoritative on the works of a slightly earlier composer.

"Let's hope that Dad doesn't know anything about it either," said Richard gloomily. Professor Crandall had trapped his host and hostess in his immediate circle, and Walter Sloane was clearly growing restive.

Walter's wife Laura was listening with a frozen smile to the details of Boccherini's early life when her stepdaughter Isabel handed her a drink.

"Thanks, sweetheart. Did you look after the others?"

"Yes."

"Oh, thanks. Listen, there's something I want to talk to you about. Excuse us for a moment, Harry."

She steered Isabel over to a corner. "Thanks for the rescue," she whispered.

"It's okay. It's better than slime molds, anyway."

"I don't know how his wife can stand it."

Isabel looked over to where the tall thin figure hovered anxiously over a tray of tempura vegetables. "She's too busy monitoring her own cholesterol level," she said.

"I had those vegetables made especially for Heather," her stepmother replied. "She won't eat meat, she won't eat fish, she won't eat caviar. She won't eat anything. Including those vegetable things. You'll see."

"I told you, she won't touch anything that's been fried."

"But darling," Laura Sloane said piteously, "if it's not meat, and it's not fried, then I ask you, what is it?"

Laura Sloane was a big good-looking woman with an easy way about her. She dominated her husband and his children so naturally that they never had time to think about or resent it. She was tall and slightly heavy, with deep-set brown eyes and honey-blonde hair. Laura was always doing big things: selling or buying companies with her father's and first husband's millions; traveling around

the world; even, in one notorious instance, hang gliding.
She had been left a widow at a young age and it had been
years before she met Walter Sloane and remarried. In
those years, she had become known for her flamboyance,
she and Freda Simms both; they had been friends since
high school. They had traveled the world, learned to
speak twelve languages between them, sailed on foreign
seas and laughed their way out of any mishap. Once, when
Laura had been dumped by a man she was seeing, she had
rented a plane and written the word BASTARD in large
plumy letters across the sky above his house. She and
Freda had the same loud laugh and the same charming
way about them. Even Laura's marriage to Walter Sloane,
three years before, had not dimmed their friendship, although it was a well-known fact that Freda hated Walter's
guts and the sentiment was warmly returned.

The adventures, however, had not continued after Laura's second marriage. She seemed at last to be settling
down.

"And the worse for it, too," Freda often said, packing
her bags to fly off to another romantic resort, silently
mourning the fact that her companion was Ted, or Eddie,
or Fred (they all seemed to have the same name) instead
of the marvelous Laura. "No spirit for adventure anymore,
that's Laura's trouble. Old Wally has sucked the blood out
of her, like the accursed vampire he is."

Freda called him Old Wally to his face, which only
served to increase the strength of the feeling between
them.

"Old bitch," Walter Sloane called her behind her back.
"Old hag."

Freda, busy with her packing, would laugh if she heard
about it.

"My mission in life," she would say, "is to make Walter Sloane uncomfortable"; and she seemed to be succeeding.

Now Laura Sloane looked around at the progress of her
party with a practiced eye. Everything was going delight-
fully well, as usual. Of course her parties always went
well. She planned them for weeks ahead of time and
everything ran like clockwork. The only problem was that
Freda, naturally, was getting drunk. So was Walter. They

both had an unfortunate tendency to drink and then to quarrel. Laura could stop her husband by taking the drink out of his hand, but she could not bring herself to do that to Freda. Freda's claim was that she never felt the liquor; no, not one bit. She said it simply made her sparkle. Laura remembered the party, in this very house, where Freda had sparkled so violently and so long that she had not been able to get out of bed for a week afterward.

"Isabel," she said now, "no more drinks for your father or Freda, okay?"

"Okay."

Isabel sat down again in the corner next to the young man she had invited. Laura regarded her stepdaughter thoughtfully. When Isabel had announced that she was bringing this friend of hers—what was his name again? Snooky? She hoped she was remembering it wrong—Laura had looked interested and asked a few questions. Who was he? Where was he from? How had they met? Isabel had smiled in that cool way of hers and said, "He's a friend—an old friend from college." Laura wondered what that meant, nowadays. Perhaps it meant that he really was just a friend. There was no telling anymore, was there? She thought he looked a trifle *young* for Isabel, who was in her mid-twenties and typically dated men ten years older than she. . . .

Laura crossed the room and took the drink out of her husband's hand, giving him a warning look as she did so. The look said, *Don't fight with me.* Of course he didn't. He just shrugged and turned away. Laura began to chat with Ruth and Sam Abrams, rescuing them from a discourse on the water resources of the Pantanal by Professor Crandall, who seemed to have worked himself up into a positive frenzy of factual information this evening.

An hour later the party began to break up. The guests drifted back and forth aimlessly, as opposed to their earlier purposeful perambulations. Heather Crandall floated over to Laura and said, "*Such* a wonderful party, as always."

"Thank you."

"We should be getting home now," said Heather, casting a faintly worried eye over to where her husband stood furiously expounding the merits of field research versus laboratory work. "Little Harry will be tired of babysitting for the other two."

Laura nodded. She suddenly felt very tired and a little sick.

"To paraphrase Alice B. Toklas," Heather Crandall said with amusement in her eye, "it will take Harry ten years to understand what he's said here tonight."

Laura looked at her sharply. Heather was Harry Crandall's third wife—or was it the fourth?—but she wasn't a fool like the others. She may have her own private obsessions about health food, but she saw her husband's more public obsessions clearly. Good for her, Laura thought wearily.

"I think I'll go upstairs and lie down," she said. "I don't feel very well. Thank you so much for coming."

"Probably something you ate," Heather said. "Remind me to talk to you about fried foods sometime."

Laura went upstairs to bed, and Walter Sloane stood by the door seeing his friends out. He came back into the living room with a smug expression on his face.

"Bunch of fools," he said to his children. Isabel's young man still lounged in the corner. "That Harry Crandall especially is an idiot. Did you hear him blowing off steam about the Pantanal? I'm sure he doesn't even know where the damned thing is. He's never even been to Argentina."

"The Pantanal," said Isabel's friend in a lordly manner, "isn't *in* Argentina."

"What?"

"It's in Brazil. In the southwest corner, to be exact. A region of swamps and flourishing animal life. Anacondas. Snails. Jaguars."

"Good Lord," said his host, giving him a frozen glance. "It's as bad as having that stuffed shirt Harry around. Where's the whiskey? Laura never lets me drink a decent amount. Whiskey, anyone?"

No one wanted any whiskey.

"Good," said Walter Sloane with satisfaction, and poured himself out a huge drink.

*   *   *

Conversations in the various cars departing from the Sloanes' house:

"That Walter," Freda Simms said with emphasis, "is an old bore. *And* a deadly miser. Did you see him watching every drink I took? What a creep. How could darling Laura have married him, I ask you? Eddie?"

Eddie shrugged. "I just met these people."

"Well, what do you think?"

Eddie maneuvered the car expertly onto the main road. "They're okay, I guess."

From there the conversation turned to his next performance at the circus and various other things. It was only when the car drove up to Freda's house that she caught herself saying with venom,

"That old hog Walter had better watch out! Did you see Harry Crandall giving him the evil eye tonight, wondering if he would pick a fight? He didn't, but only because of Laura, poor dear. Old Wally had better watch out—someone's going to do it in for him one of these days!"

In the Crandalls' car Heather was saying fretfully,

"I *told* her *never* to eat anything that's been fried in oil. Really, the only cooking oil that's suitable for frying is Indian *ghee*. You know. It's stable at high temperatures and—"

"Did you see Walter's face when I was talking about the resources of the Pantanal?" said Professor Crandall, following his own train of thought. "I'll bet he doesn't even know where the Pantanal is. Don't you think so, darling?"

"Yes, Harry," Heather said submissively.

"Ignoramus," her husband said gleefully. "That's what he is, you know, Heather. A total ignoramus."

"Yes, darling."

"What were you and Laura talking about?"

"She wasn't feeling well. I was going to tell her about *ghee* but I didn't have the time."

"Oh, well. Next time, then."

"Yes," said Heather. "Next time."

*　　*　　*

In the Abramses' car the conversation was short and direct.

"That Freda," Sam Abrams was saying. He was a little gray man with a resigned expression. "Has she ever had a day's worry in her life?"

"Oh, Sam, that's not fair," said Ruth. "Her husband died."

"And left her with more money than she knows what to do with."

"Oh, Sam."

Her husband gave her a quizzical glance. "You wouldn't think of knocking me off, now would you, honey? For the insurance money, maybe?"

"Oh, *Sam.*" Ruth felt resentful. You shouldn't even joke about things like that, her expression said.

But it was true enough, what he had said about Freda Simms. Not that she had had such an easy time of it—look at the way she drank, she certainly had her share of problems. She was running away from *something.* But she had never had to worry about money.

Ruth felt that awful feeling again, that stab of resentment. She had never had to *worry.* . . .

Isabel Sloane saw her friend out to his car.

"Snooky," she said, "it was terrific seeing you again. How long will you be at your sister's?"

"About as long as she and her husband can stand me."

"Let's get together soon."

The young man looked down at her thoughtfully. "Why don't you come over for dinner tomorrow night?"

"Your sister wouldn't mind?"

"Oh, no. She and Bernard love that kind of thing."

"Well . . . okay. That would be great. See you then."

She stood and watched as he drive away. She didn't wave.

On the way home he punched the radio dials aimlessly. Finally, giving up, he began to whistle an opera aria. He was singing by the time he reached his sister's house and roaring as he climbed the front steps.

His sister came out on the porch and flicked on the light.

"So there you are, you slobhead," she said affectionately.

"Here I am, myself."

"Have fun at your party?"

"Uh-huh. Hey, Maya?"

"Speak on, little one."

"You wouldn't mind having Isabel over for dinner tomorrow, would you?"

"Oh, no," said his sister, flicking off the porch light and closing the door. "You know I just live to entertain your little friends."

*   *   *

"Sam," Ruth Abrams said, "Sam, where's the sugar bowl?"

She was standing on a chair and reaching into the dark recesses of the upper shelf of the pantry.

"Sam?"

Her husband had disappeared somewhere, probably into the basement to tinker with the old radios and dinosaurlike remnants of electrical equipment he hoarded down there.

Ruth did what she always did in these cases. She raised her voice and bellowed at the top of her lungs,

"*SAM?*"

The pantry rattled and the cat scuttled away, but there was no answer from below. Ruth sighed and scrabbled about among the items on the shelf.

Something would have to be done about this pantry, she thought, as she always did when forced to find something. Just look at this. Old half-used containers of oatmeal (probably maggoty by now), sticky bottles of jam with the contents ossified beyond recognition, envelopes of instant soup mix, decades old. In fact, the whole thing could be reorganized as a kind of museum of how her children lived twenty years ago. And the sugar bowl nowhere to be seen.

Well, she would just have to use something else in that cake batter. She descended from the chair and looked thoughtfully into the mixing bowl. How about maple syrup, or honey? Sam wouldn't mind. Or how about that stuff her

friend Heather Crandall had given her weeks ago . . .
where was it now . . . on the bottom shelf under the
sink . . . ?

She emerged from her search triumphantly this time,
her face flushed and gray hair tousled, holding a jar of
brown rice syrup. She looked at it doubtfully. "Far better
for you than sugar," Heather had said, pressing it into her
hands. "Trust me. It's made up of maltose and other
complex sugars. It's not nearly as—as *aggressive* as table
sugar. Try it."

Ruth had never thought of ordinary sugar as particularly hostile, but she supposed it could be. She stood in
the middle of the kitchen, turning the jar over and over in
her hands. She was a short plump woman in her early
sixties with a mop of graying curls and a humble, anxious
expression. Well, of course Heather always knew best
about cookery. Heather would bake a cake using this
strange syrupy stuff, and it would turn out delicious—her
cakes always did. Ruth was miserably aware that the same

was not true for her. She tried to copy Heather and turn out gourmet meals (how Heather did it, from carrot scrapings and turtle beans, Ruth could never quite figure out), but somehow the result was never the same. She gazed earnestly at the syrup, which had a pleasing golden color like honey, and sighed. Well, Heather knew best.

The phone rang and she picked it up, absentmindedly unscrewing the top of the jar and tilting it over the mixing bowl.

"Hello?"

It was Heather. Her voice sounded strange; rusty, almost.

"What?" said Ruth vaguely. She could never take in things quickly at the best of times. It was something everyone knew about her. "Poor Ruth," they said, "not too quick, is she?"

"Ruth," Heather said with a choking sound, "Ruthie, I'm telling you, Laura Sloane is dead. She's *dead*!"

"She can't be," Ruth said slowly, in her hesitant way. "She was—she was fine last night."

"She was *not*. She didn't feel well when we left. And then it came on her in the middle of the night—some sort of stroke or heart attack, we don't know which—"

"Laura? *Laura*?"

Heather sighed impatiently. "Ruth. Please. Pull yourself together. Go tell Sam. We'll have to go over to the house—bring flowers or something—"

"Yes," said Ruth. "Yes. Yes, we will. Flowers would be nice."

She hung up and stood there uncertainly. Her mind was going round and round; how could this . . . how could this happen . . . how could this happen . . . !

All at once her attention was diverted by more mundane matters.

"Oh, *hell*," she said firmly.

The syrup jar she was holding was empty; and now the cake mix would be very sweet indeed.

Snooky and his sister Maya were having a busy Sunday morning. They sat amidst the wreckage of their brunch.

Maya and her husband Bernard were doing the crossword puzzle.

"Six letters," Maya was saying. "A hollow cylinder."

"A hollow cylinder," mused Bernard. He was a large man with intelligent brown eyes, dark curly hair and a beard; he looked like an amicable bear. "I don't know. How about this one? 'The stalk of an ovule.' Any guesses?"

There was silence around the table.

"Gabion," said Snooky, not looking up from the morning paper. He was reading the cartoon page as intently as if it were the News of the Week in Review.

"Excuse me?"

"Gabion."

"Which one?" asked Maya.

"Hollow cylinder."

"Thanks."

"No problem."

There was another silence.

"Funiculus," said Snooky.

"The stalk of an ovule?" said Maya.

"Yes."

"It fits," she said excitedly. "Hey, Snookers. How about 'an extensive plain, in Spain?' Five letters."

Her brother turned a page. "Llano," he said. "L-L-A-N-O."

"Thanks."

"You're welcome."

"This is no fun at all," said Bernard dispiritedly. "Where's the challenge?"

"Snooky's always been good at crossword puzzles. Don't take it personally, Bernard."

Bernard subsided into an unhappy silence. Snooky raised a warning eyebrow at his sister.

Maya was five years older, but other than that they looked very much alike. Both were lanky, with pale faces, thin crooked noses and straight golden-brown hair which Maya wore in a pageboy and Snooky wore carelessly brushed back. They were fine-boned and aristocratic-looking, like greyhounds.

"Be careful, darling sister. You're going to sour my visit here."

He had shown up at their door with little or no advance warning only a week before. His full name was Arthur B. Randolph, and he had no occupation. Maya looked over at him fondly. He was their elder brother William's greatest failure; William, who was ten years older than Maya and had single-handedly raised the two of them after their parents died. William, the lawyer, who had tried to instill the work ethic into each of his younger siblings and had succeeded only with Maya, who had a job writing a weekly column for a magazine called *The Animal World*. She wrote on subjects varying from the denizens of the Amazon to the possibility of life in outer space. Snooky referred to it as "the jungle beetle column"; he was vaguely scornful of her career, but then, of course, Snooky had never worked a day in his life. William had nearly broken down on that momentous day, four years ago, when Snooky had reached the age of twenty-one and William had been forced to give him his share of their parents' wealth.

"Wastrel," William had told Maya, tears streaming down his face. She had never seen him so upset. "Wastrel! He'll go straight through it. You'll see, Maya. He'll squander it all."

But Snooky had not squandered it. For the past four years he had roamed the country, settling first here, then there, flitting from place to place like a large good-natured dragonfly. One of his favorite places to visit was his sister's sprawling Victorian house in Ridgewood, Connecticut. Ridgewood was a lovely little town that had retained some of its original New England charm; it had a quiet Main Street lined with shops and was surrounded by lakes and wooded hills. It was just over two hours away from New York City and featured what Bernard prized most in life: seclusion.

"Sometimes I think," Maya had remarked to Snooky once, "if Bernard could be a hermit and still be married, he would be."

"I don't know what you're talking about, Maya. Bernard *is* a married hermit."

Bernard and Maya had purchased the house four years earlier, when they got married. They had fallen in love with it at first sight, much as they had with each other (both were firm believers in intuition), and had bought it over the objections of their friend and real estate agent, a short surly individual named Seymour. Seymour had pointed out the many disadvantages: the plumbing, in a sad state of disrepair; the huge heating bills; the window on the third floor in the back bedroom which would have to be fixed; the cold drafts through the ridiculous number of fireplaces (five). What Maya and Bernard had seen was a beautiful old house on a winding lane, with an expanse of green lawn, a patch of woods, and the nearest house, a geodesic dome made primarily of glass, far enough away for privacy.

"I won't let you buy it," Seymour had announced in a menacing manner. "It'll fall down. You'll live to regret it. Trust me. It's my business."

"We're buying it," Bernard said. Bernard, in general, spoke very little; this was a long sentence for him.

"You're not."

"We are."

"Over my dead body," said Seymour.

Bernard shrugged. "Get the gun," he said to Maya.

They settled the contract and moved in in record time. It turned out that Seymour had been wrong about nearly everything. The house was a little cold in winter, but the addition of a new and larger furnace took care of that problem, and within a year they had turned it into a comfortable, even luxurious, home. The sun room was filled with flowering plants and vines; the living room had leaded-glass windows and a window seat piled high with pillows. The dining room contained sturdy antique mahogany and oak furniture (Bernard, while not overweight, was heavily built and had managed to destroy an expensive French armchair simply by sitting down on it). Maya filled the house with unusual pieces of sculpture, odds and ends picked up at antique sales, and bright Navajo rugs.

"It's too comfortable," Bernard would say whenever company arrived. Bernard hated company. "Too damn comfortable. Turn the heat down, Maya. Let them suffer."

One visitor whom Bernard regarded with somewhat less than his usual animosity was Snooky, who showed up at random intervals and appropriated for himself the small bedroom on the third floor at the back. He arrived with little or no baggage, ate huge amounts of their food and borrowed freely from Bernard's wardrobe. He would leave just as suddenly as he arrived, getting on the plane to some distant place; his ambition was to live for a while in every state in the U.S., although he tended to shy away from the general vicinity of southern California, where his brother William lived. Over the years William and his stiff unbending wife, Emily, had issued warnings, then denunciations, then messages of despair and entreaty concerning Snooky's lifestyle. William's favorite phrase was "Think of Mother."

"I think," Snooky said one day, seated on the porch of yet another of his rented homes, "I *think* Mother would have wanted me to be happy. Don't you agree, Maya?"

There was no doubt that whatever his mother might have wanted, Snooky was content with his life. He had plenty of money, he moved from place to place, he met all kinds of people and went everywhere. It suited him down to the ground.

William would make a sad mooing sound whenever the subject of Snooky came up.

"*Tramp*," he would say with a kind of grisly pleasure. "Tramp. That's what he is. I predicted it, Maya. I predicted it."

His wife went even further.

"Good-for-nothing," she would say tartly. "Jack of all trades and master of none. A roamer, a wastrel, a flibbertigibbet."

Having relieved herself of these platitudes, she would nod firmly and turn away before Maya had a chance to say anything in her brother's defense.

"That's not true at all," Snooky would say when he heard of this. "I'm not a jack of *any* trade."

Now this object of loathing and scorn scanned the newspaper and finally put it down with a sigh.

"If you ask me," he said, "this paper doesn't have enough cartoons. Not nearly enough."

"I just got thirty-one across, Maya," said Bernard.

"Really?" She craned her neck to see. "What was it?"

" 'Evoke.' "

"Oh, okay. 'Evoke.' That means fifteen down must start with a K. Damn. I thought it was 'anti.' "

"Fascinating though this is," Snooky said, folding the paper into a large lopsided hat, "I have to go. Remember, Isabel's coming over for dinner."

"That's right. Your girlfriend."

"She's not my girlfriend. She was never my girlfriend. We were just friends in college. I tried my best to improve on the relationship, but she wasn't interested. She's a couple of years older than me. I was a sophomore when she was a senior." Snooky cheerfully unfolded and refolded the hat.

"The unbridgeable social abyss," said Maya.

"That's right."

A few days after Snooky's arrival Maya had sent him out to a fashionable little grocery store called, quaintly, the European Common Market. There were many stores of this kind in Ridgewood; specialty stores where brie was sold strictly by the wheel, five different kinds of water-decaffeinated coffee beans were readily available, and suburban matrons in black leather pants could be seen leaning over the cheese counter and crying, "What do you *mean* the Cambozolla is overripe?" Snooky loved to shop there. He was holding a cranshaw melon and watching two women get into a heated argument with the store manager, apparently over a lost charge card (money, actual money, was never in evidence at the European Common Market; instead, customers wielded their own pink charge cards), when someone had called out his name. It was Isabel. It turned out she lived nearby. They hadn't seen each other since college but she was unchanged; as beautiful as ever.

"You'll see, you'll like her," Snooky said. "Both of you. Even Bernard, who hates everyone. You don't know her parents, do you? No? You'll see, Maya. You'll get a chance to tell her what a terrible person I am. You can get out William's letters and read from them for evidence. You and Bernard will tell her everything about me, and she'll tell you all about herself, and you'll end up the best of friends while I sit there silently, saying nothing."

"Remember the lamb chops, while you're out," Maya said absently. Her mind was on the crossword puzzle.

Bernard said, "I have to go, too, Maya. I have some work to finish up."

"Don't go, Bernard. Don't leave me here alone with all these blank spaces left."

He wavered visibly. "But I have a chapter due."

Bernard was also a writer. He wrote children's books about rats, mice and talking sheep. His sheep books were the most popular; Mrs. Woolly, a maternal ewe with wire-rimmed spectacles and a careworn but kindly face, was well-known in households with children aged seven and under.

"And I have an article due," said Maya. "It doesn't matter. Stay just a little."

The telephone rang. Snooky paused by the hallway mirror to adjust his paper hat, then went upstairs and picked up the phone.

"What? Slow down, Isabel . . . what? *What?* Oh my God . . . all right. Yes. I'll be right over. Of course. Anything I can bring or do? Okay. Ten minutes."

He rushed downstairs past Maya and Bernard, who had their heads together over the puzzle.

He shouted something and the front door slammed.

Maya and Bernard looked at each other.

"That's your brother," said Bernard. "Honestly. Always rushing in and out."

"He's crazy," Maya said. "I love him, but he's a crazy person. Bernard, what's an eight-letter word for 'May fly'?"

Freda Simms put down the phone. Isabel had called her after the long night at the hospital. Of course it was natural that she would call her; she was Laura's best friend. And as much as she hated Walter Sloane, she had always liked his two kids.

Freda sat staring at the wall for a long time. She felt calm; very calm. How could this have happened to Laura? Poison, the doctors had said. *Poison.* Who would want to poison darling Laura?

She lowered her head into her hands. She suddenly felt very tired. So tired . . . Her head drooped and her face looked very old. Her artificially bright hair hung over her forehead and she brushed it away with an impatient gesture.

Something to drink . . . She got up, went into the kitchen and poured herself a drink. Some whiskey would be nice. Yes. She went back and sat down again, staring at the wall.

There was a crash and she looked around in bewilderment. It was her drink . . . the glass had shattered against the wall. She must have thrown it. She didn't remember. She didn't remember . . . !

Oh, God! Now there would be all that glass to clean up. And the dark stain of whiskey all over her nice new Persian rug.

Who . . . who would want to kill darling Laura?

"An organophosphate poison," said the doctor, reading from the chart. He was young and had kind, tired eyes. "Some form of anticholinesterase. In plain language?"

"Yes," said Detective Jim Voelker.

"Insecticide. A strong solution. In something she drank last night. The first symptoms should appear an hour, maybe an hour and a half after ingestion."

"Anything you could do?"

The doctor shook his head. "She didn't get here until two o'clock. By the time we began the treatment it was already too late. We did all we could, but—"

"Yes," said Voelker. "Thank you. I may need to talk to you again later."

The doctor nodded and moved off. He looked like he could use some sleep, Voelker thought.

Jim Voelker was a quiet, morose-looking man in his early forties with short graying hair and a solemn expression. He shook his head and consulted his notes. Seemed pretty straightforward. Woman was poisoned last night at a party in her home. Her husband found her in convulsions when he went upstairs; he rushed her to the hospital, where she died shortly afterwards. The only thing unusual about it was the husband's story. Usually the husband claimed to know nothing about it. Sometimes they did, sometimes they didn't. Voelker looked at his notes with interest. This time the husband insisted that the poisoned drink was meant for *him*. Was quite definite about it, according to these notes, hastily put together for him by one of his subordinates.

Voelker's habitually morose face grew longer and sadder. Inside, however, what he felt was a spark of anticipation.

He would have to talk to this husband, what's his name, Sloane—yes. He would have to talk to everybody on this list. Everyone who was at that party last night, everyone they knew, everyone who knew the Sloanes. He wondered if they had been happy. Perhaps they were. His mind lingered with a moment's passing regret on that circumstance, hypothetical though it might be; then he shrugged it off. Voelker was not the kind to dwell on hypothetical circumstances and regrets. He wanted to meet these people and hear what they had to say.

And what they *didn't* have to say. Yes. After so many years as a detective, he could hear that almost as well. He nodded to himself in satisfaction. He wanted to find out all about these people!

2

"Bernard," said Maya, "did you hear what Snooky just told me?"

"What is it?"

"The hostess of that party he went to last night—well, she died. They say she was *poisoned*."

Bernard looked up from his desk. "You're kidding."

"No."

"That's horrible." Bernard felt strangely offended. Murders, he felt, should not happen in his vicinity.

"Well, he's pretty upset."

"Mmm-hmmm. Do you think he did it?"

"Bernard, please."

"I suppose this means the police will be here to question him."

"I guess so. I don't know. It's not like he *knew* any of those people, really. He just met them last night." Maya perched miserably on the edge of the chair and her husband put his arm around her.

"This is awful," she said. "I mean, Snooky is always getting into some kind of trouble, but he never actually ran afoul of the law before. I'm worried about him."

"Sweetheart, your brother did not murder his hostess last night. The police must know that. All the same—"

"What?"

"All the same, I wonder who did," said Bernard.

* * *

22

"*Honestly*," said Ruth Abrams, shutting the door on Detective Voelker's departing back, "he might just as well have come out and accused us of doing it, Sam!"

"It's his manner," said her husband mildly. "The man has an unfortunate manner."

Voelker had sat looking very mournful and considerate and asking all sorts of prying questions. How long had they known Walter and Laura Sloane? What, in their opinion, was the Sloanes' relationship like? How did Walter and Laura get along with his two children? About the party the night before: did they have anything to drink? Did they see Laura taking a drink? How about Walter? And most importantly, did they see Laura taking a drink out of her husband's hand?

Ruth had sat straight upright and answered the questions as factually as she could. All the while she had felt a growing sense of alarm. How could the police be sitting here, right in her living room, asking all these questions? How could this thing have happened?

Sam had not liked it much, either. Yes, he said matter-of-factly, he worked for Walter Sloane. Yes, he was his second-in-command. It was a consulting firm. Small business analyses, computer work, some accounting and survey work. He and Ruth had known Walter for years; twenty, perhaps thirty years. They had known Laura only three years, since Walter married her. How did Walter and Laura get along? Great, as far as he could tell. And Walter's two kids liked his new wife, too. There were none of the usual stepmother problems. Of course Isabel was already an adult when her father remarried.

The party last night? It was like any other party. Yes, there was some drinking; there always was. No, they hadn't seen Laura taking a drink from Walter, although she sometimes did that when he had had too much. Did he often drink too much? Sometimes . . . not often. He wasn't an alcoholic, if that's what the detective meant.

Voelker looked more mournful than ever. No, he wasn't implying that anyone was an alcoholic. He just wanted the facts. He had spoken to Walter Sloane and his children already, and after this interview he would go on to the Crandalls' house. They must understand, it was his job to talk to everyone who was at that party last night. They did understand?

Sam had said well, of course, naturally.

Good, said Voelker. Now, about your consulting business, Mr. Abrams . . .

When he went on his way, he had two new facts to think about. One was that the Abramses had not actually seen Laura Sloane take a drink from her husband's hand. That was Sloane's story: that the insecticide was meant for him, but Laura must have taken the glass from his hand and drunk it instead. Pretty weak story, in Voelker's opinion. The second fact was that Sam Abrams was in a very interesting position relative to Walter Sloane. He was vice-president of their small business. That meant that if Sloane died or was disabled, Sam Abrams would take over.

Voelker sat in his car and flipped through his notes. He recalled his visit to the Sloane house. Mansion, rather. Walter and Laura Sloane lived in a semi-regal style, in a white mansion at the top of a hill, at the end of a long tree-lined drive. The house was built in a U around an open courtyard where a single cherry tree bloomed. Inside, the rooms were furnished in pale creams and grays; Laura Sloane's taste must have been modern, tending toward chairs that looked like plastic globes and tables made of steel and glass. Voelker shook his head. You couldn't even see the house from the road, for Christ's sake. It sat grandly on top of its own hill, surrounded by trees, like a castle. Voelker had lived and worked in Ridgewood for a long time, and certainly not all of it was that wealthy, but there were some areas, bastions of old money, that still amazed him. Somebody was certainly loaded. It turned out it had been Laura; she was the (he consulted his notes) Wuff-Wuff Dog Chow heiress. Voelker chewed his lip thoughtfully. He had raised his own dog, Angles, on Wuff-Wuff Dog Chow. Good stuff. Angles had certainly been crazy about it. So that was Laura Sloane's father, was it? Lots of money there. And her first husband had been loaded, too.

Walter Sloane had said quite frankly that his wife's money was going to him for his lifetime; then to the two kids. The will had not yet been read, but that was the gist of it. And then, in the same breath, Sloane had denied any intention to murder his wife for her money. Throughout the interview, he had claimed that someone was trying to murder *him*.

Voelker thought of him: the grizzled hair, the sharp blue eyes, the gaunt body, aggressive and strong. Sloane had a long thin face and hands that moved rapidly as he talked. He seemed tired and belligerent. He had endured the interview for as long as he could, and then at the end had roused himself and snapped, "That's enough, damn you," leaving the room without a backward glance.

Pugnacious, thought Voelker. That was the word. Pugnacious. Difficult. Not to his wife, though; so far the consensus was clear about that. She could tame him with just a look.

After him, Voelker had interviewed the two children. Richard was startlingly handsome, with his fair hair and chiseled features, but at the time Voelker saw him he was hollow-eyed from lack of sleep and his mouth was set in a frown. He slumped listlessly in his chair and said he hadn't seen anything. He had gone to the party because he had nothing else to do and it was in his own home, wasn't it? He had sat in the corner all evening. He had talked to his sister and his sister's friend. He hadn't seen any hocus-pocus with the drinks. He hadn't seen *anything*. Could he go now?

His sister, Isabel, was different. She was subdued, still in shock, but in very good control of herself. She too had been up all the previous night, but her pale face was freshly washed and her hair was pulled back neatly with a blue velvet ribbon. She had sat upright, crossed her legs, lit a cigarette and answered all of Voelker's questions coolly, almost indifferently.

Yes, she had helped with the drinks. She always did that. People expected it. She didn't mind. Yes, she and Richard always got along fine with their stepmother. What did he mean? No, there was no trouble between them. Oh, well, Daddy was another matter.

Yes, thought Voelker. Walter Sloane was always another matter. Everyone he had seen so far had expressed amazement that Laura would be a victim of murder. Everyone had hinted that they would have been far less amazed had the corpse been that of her husband.

Isabel had shrugged. Well, Daddy was a difficult person.

Did he have enemies? Voelker wanted to know.

Well, yes, she said. He had a tendency to be a little— well, a little *abrasive*.

Yes, thought Voelker. A little abrasive. It was a masterful understatement.

Isabel didn't know anything in particular against her father's friends. She had known them all her life and couldn't say a bad word against them. She looked at him calmly and lit another cigarette.

Voelker gazed into those steely blue eyes and thought he could see a faint resemblance between Isabel Sloane and her father. They didn't look alike, but the ice-blue eyes and the cold angles of the face were the same.

"How old are you, Miss Sloane?"

Isabel lifted her eyebrows at this. "I'm twenty-seven."

"Do you have an apartment elsewhere, or do you live here?"

"I live here," she said flatly.

"And what kind of work do you do?"

It turned out that Isabel did not work. She had never worked. She had come home when she graduated from college and had cooked and cleaned for her brother and father—and, for the last few years, his new wife—since then.

"I don't mind," she said. "I'd rather do what I'm doing than work. I'm not cut out for nine-to-five."

"I see."

Isabel looked at him steadily at that point and said that she had a lot of work to do now, as a matter of fact, and she hadn't had any sleep last night. So if the interview was over . . . ?

Yes, said Voelker. The interview was over.

"Please, Inspector," said Heather Crandall, pushing the cup toward Detective Voelker. "Have another cup of my blackstrap molasses drink."

"No, thank you, ma'am," said Voelker, casting a frightened look at the oily black liquid. "It was very good, ma'am, thank you. And I'm not an inspector. Just a detective."

"Oh yes, that's English, isn't it? Please, detective or lieutenant or whatever you are, have another cup. It's awfully good for you."

"No, thank you."

"Blackstrap molasses," said Heather reprovingly, "is an excellent source of calcium."

"Yes, ma'am."

"And iron."

"Yes, ma'am."

In an effort to regain control of the interview, Voelker shuffled his notes. He looked through them anxiously, then rose from the table.

"Thank you, Mrs. Crandall, Professor Crandall. I may need to speak to you again at a later date," he said in his most formal manner. It was meant to head off any inclination that woman might have to make another one of those godawful drinks.

"Good-bye, Officer."

"Good-bye."

Harry closed the door behind the departing policeman and returned to the table. Heather was stirring her molasses drink idly with a spoon and smiling to herself.

"Awfully good," she murmured, "or just plain awful?"

"What, darling?"

"Nothing. What did you think of that, Harry?"

Harry Crandall sat down and lit his pipe. He was a short, balding man who couldn't think at all without his pipe. Heather had tried in vain for years and years to get him to stop. It was a hopeless task.

"My pipe and I," he would say menacingly, "are as one."

"Oh, Harry. It's *so* bad for you. Your lungs . . ."

"I don't inhale it."

"Freud," Heather would say solemnly, "died of throat cancer. Freud smoked a pipe."

"Freud was one of the greatest geniuses of the twentieth century. Freud smoked a pipe."

"Oh, *Harry.*"

"Or was it cigars Freud smoked?" mused her husband.

Heather would shrug. She was not interested. This was the kind of detail that Harry prided himself on knowing, but no one else cared about.

"The point is, Harry," she would say firmly, "he *smoked.*"

Now her husband, ignoring her mute look of protest,

lit the tobacco and puffed. The pipe went out. He lit it again and puffed vigorously. Heather watched disapprovingly. Harry loved this little ritual. He maintained that the look of pained dismay she gave him every time improved the flavor.

"What do you think, Harry?" she repeated.

"I think that policeman is wondering why we don't seem more broken up over this."

Heather stirred the blackstrap molasses vigorously. "We didn't know Laura that well," she pointed out. "Just the past couple of years or so. While you've known Walter—?"

"Nearly thirty years."

"It's a tragedy, of course. A real tragedy. I sent flowers to the house and I'm going over there tomorrow with Ruth."

"That's nice."

Little Harry came in, pulled out a chair and sat down. The chair groaned audibly but did not give way.

Little Harry was Heather and Harry Crandall's eldest son. He was seventeen years old and well over six feet. Heather didn't know how much he weighed these days, but it was a steadily increasing number that always seemed to be evenly divisible by ten. Little Harry was not fat. He was a solid mass of muscle. He was the high school football coach's favorite human being. His full name was Harold A. Crandall, Jr., but he had been called Little Harry for so long that the name had ceased to have any meaning and had become a sort of tag. He had passed his father's height and weight around age twelve and continued to sprout upward. It was a wonder to all their friends that on a diet of vegetables, rice, tofu and miso soup, Little Harry grew as he did.

"She must be doing something right," Freda had said grudgingly. "Just *look* at that kid."

Ruth Abrams was in awe of him. Her own son, Jonathan, was ten years older than Little Harry (Heather was the youngest of their group and her children were a full generation behind everyone else's), but he was a little runt who weighed in at five foot ten, a hundred and fifty pounds. Jonathan claimed he made up for this by intellectual power—he had based his life and self-respect on this theory—but Ruth was still overwhelmed by the prodigious size of Heather's offspring.

"It's like Melvin's favorite story," she would say. Melvin was her five-year-old grandson. "Little Harry is like Jack and the Beanstalk *all in one.*"

Now Little Harry grinned at his parents. "Where's the chow?"

"Dinner's not ready yet," said Heather.

Little Harry looked distressed. He put his hand on his stomach.

"But I'm *hungry.*"

"Eat this," said Heather, with the patience born of long experience.

Little Harry took the carrot she handed him, rose, and wandered out of the room. Heather watched him go with pride in her eyes

"Our son," she often said, "is living proof that athletes can thrive on a meatless diet."

Heather was a strict vegetarian. She was anti-meat, anti-flesh foods, anti-sugar. She believed in the regenerative powers of whole foods, fresh dairy products and carob powder.

"Harry," she said now, "do you think you should have told that detective about how you fight with Walter?"

Her husband puffed away complacently.

"Don't be silly, Heather. I have nothing to hide. He asked me about my relationship with Sloane, and so I told him. I'm his first wife's cousin. So what? Sloane is a self-satisfied, egotistical bastard. I don't know why I've stayed friends with him all these years."

Because you love to argue with him, Heather longed to say, but she stopped herself. Harry would not enjoy that piece of self-knowledge. The two men loved to bicker over the stupidest things. And sometimes the fights got really acrimonious. There was that argument two weeks ago at the tennis party—Heather had thought they would come to blows. Just lucky that the policeman hadn't asked about *that.*

Charlie, her ten-year-old, came into the kitchen.

"Mom. I'm hungry."

Charlie was a thin whining child who wore glasses and threatened to take after his father. He loved to lecture his friends and boss them around. He was a normal height for his age, but next to his older brother's prodigious growth he looked practically stunted. He lived in Little Harry's oversized shadow; it covered him like a huge blanket.

"Can I have something before dinner?"

"What do you want?" asked Heather, fearing the answer.

"Candy," said Charlie promptly.

"You can have a carrot."

"Oh, all *right*."

With Charlie safely out of the way, Heather said, "But darling, who in the world would want to poison Laura? Everyone at that party last night was friends with her. Everyone *liked* her, for God's sake."

"We don't know that," her husband said, his mild blue eyes meeting hers. "We don't know that. There may have been—Secret Grudges."

He said it very self-importantly, in capital letters.

Heather pondered this. Secret grudges? But *who*? Of course she knew there were some bad feelings and resentments—there were bound to be, among any group of friends. But what was Harry saying? Did he know something she didn't?

She lifted herself gracefully out of the chair and set about preparing dinner. Heather was tall and willowy, with long brown hair parted in the middle and a pale intelligent face. She was in her early forties, nearly two decades younger than her husband and his group of friends, and some of them thought she was flaky because of her preoccupation with the proper kinds of food. She wasn't, of course. No, she wasn't. The only one who recognized that was Ruth, poor muddleheaded old Ruth, so eager to copy what Heather did. And yet, mused Heather, Ruth was the only one who had befriended her in the beginning, when she was a 23-year-old graduate student who had suddenly married her own advisor. Professor Harry Crandall had been a middle-aged man reeling from his third divorce, and Heather, who always knew exactly what she wanted when she saw it, had carefully and competently reeled him in. She could still remember the cookies Ruth had baked for her—those awful cookies, little gooey messes or dried-up rocks—and the pathetic little cakes Ruth had brought by when they were just becoming friends. At the time, Harry's favorite cousin had been married to Walter Sloane, and Sloane and Sam Abrams were in business together, so the three couples had formed a group.

"But, darling—" Heather was saying, chopping broccoli into little florets, when their youngest son came into the room. He looked up at his mother with round blue eyes.

"Mommy?"

"Yes, sweetheart?"

"I'm hungry."

"Applesauce?"

He thought this over carefully.

"Okay."

She took out a little bowl and spooned some of her homemade applesauce (no refined sugar, no artificial ingredients) into it. Linus took it and sat down under the table at his father's feet. He took the little plastic spoon she gave him and began to eat greedily.

She glanced down at him lovingly. Her baby! Linus was only five years old, but already he promised to be another Little Harry. He was big for his age and strong, and he ate *everything*, absolutely everything. They had named him after Linus Pauling, one of Harry's idols. "The greatest chemist of his time," Harry said. "One of the greatest scientists of his generation."

Heather hadn't really liked the name, but she hadn't wanted to disagree too violently. After all, Linus could always change it or take a nickname when he got older.

Now Linus sat under the table and gobbled his applesauce while Heather continued with her train of thought.

"So you think someone had a secret grudge against the Sloanes?" she asked.

"Well, what do you think?"

"Ye-e-es," said Heather slowly. "Yes. I don't know."

"Against Laura . . . or against Walter."

Heather nodded. "Yes. Walter." They exchanged meaningful glances. "He's so difficult," she continued. "Of course I've always liked him because of how wonderful he is with Linus, but . . ."

"He's a difficult man. Impossible, in fact."

"Yes. I suppose people are jealous of his money."

Her husband tamped down his pipe. "That's true. He was never wealthy before he married Laura. Wuff-Wuff Dog Chow; that stuff is worth a fortune, an absolute fortune. Walter never made much with his business."

"Look at how Ruth and Sam live."

"Scrimping and saving," said her husband. "Scrimping and saving."

"While all the while Walter lives in luxury." Heather fell silent. She took an onion and neatly peeled and sliced it.

Secret grudges? Was that one of them?

At the next house Detective Voelker visited, a white Victorian with blue trim, the door was opened by a large man who stared at him in a suspicious manner.

"Mr. Arthur Randolph?" said Voelker.

"God forbid."

Voelker consulted his notes. "Mr. Woodruff? Mr. Bernard Woodruff?"

"Yes." Bernard leaned back and shouted, "*Snooky!*"

After Snooky ushered the detective into the living room, Bernard went back into the kitchen and said to his wife, "This is nice. Your brother has been here a little over a week and he's already managed to involve us with the Law."

"It's not his fault, Bernard. He can't help it if he was invited to that party."

"I told him not to go."

"You always tell everybody not to go anywhere. Other

people enjoy parties. Not everyone is like you." Maya leaned into the dining room and whistled for the dog. "Misty? Misty? Where *is* that dog?"

Misty, a small red mop of mixed origins, crept into the kitchen, sensing the tense atmosphere.

"I have an idea," said Bernard. "Why don't we write to your brother William and tell him that Snooky is a murder suspect?"

"Is that supposed to be helpful?" she snapped.

In the living room, Detective Voelker was saying, "Your full name is Arthur B. Randolph?"

"That's right."

"What does the B stand for?"

"Nothing. It's a rudimentary appendage. Like an appendix. It's there, you know, but what does it do?"

Voelker regarded him thoughtfully. "What time did you arrive at the Sloane home last night?"

"Around eight o'clock."

The list of questions went on—a long list. Snooky answered each question promptly. Voelker left three quarters of an hour later. Snooky closed the door and went down the hallway to the kitchen, where he found Bernard hovering over the stove, stirring what looked like a cauldron of brown sludge. Snooky was intrigued.

"What's that, Bernard?"

"I'm not sure."

"What's it supposed to be?"

"Indian pudding."

"Looks like glue."

"You're having it for dessert."

"Oh."

The kitchen was country-style, with a heavy oak table in the center, copper pots hanging from the walls and ceiling, and wooden counters on three sides of the room. Maya was poking around in the pantry, a separate alcove off to one side. "Where's the beans?" she yelled now.

"The what?" Bernard shouted.

"The *beans!*"

Snooky picked up a can from the table. "Here, Maya."

"Oh." Maya came in and gave him a curious glance. "You okay, Snooks?"

"It's a humbling experience, being interviewed by the police. It's never happened to me before."

"I find that hard to believe," said Bernard.

Snooky leaned against the wall and crossed his arms. "Isabel's in a bad fix. I'm worried about her, My. Whoever did this could care less about the kind of trouble it gets her into."

Maya regarded him soberly. "I'm more worried about the trouble *you're* getting into, Snooks."

"Oh, I'm okay. I'm always okay. You know that." Snooky helped carry the food into the dining room, then sat down and played moodily with the three-bean salad on his plate.

"What did that detective ask you?" Bernard wanted to know.

"Oh, you know. The usual stuff. What I saw, who I talked to. Nothing that would interest *you*, Bernard. Nothing to do with sheep or rats."

These were the species that, blessed with the gift of speech and rational thought, figured prominently in Bernard's books.

"It so happens that many things interest me," said Bernard stiffly.

Snooky did not reply. He was going over things in his head.

Who at that party had a good reason to murder Laura Sloane?

Driving away from the house, Voelker was turning over the interview in his mind.

The young man didn't know the first thing about it. He felt sure of that. He had answered all of Voelker's questions clearly and intelligently. And he had told Voelker something that no one else had seen, something that the detective found very interesting.

Yes, he said, Laura Sloane had crossed the room once, on purpose, to take a drink out of her husband's hand. He had seen it. No, probably no one else had. The guests were all laughing and talking in little groups. Why would they pay attention? He had seen it because Laura had just finished talking to his friend Isabel. Laura had broken off

her conversation and set out purposefully across the room
to get that drink.

Why? Voelker had asked.

The young man had shrugged. Her husband was getting a little drunk, maybe a little obnoxious. Or was about
to. His eyes had followed her because—because she seemed
so *determined*. Everyone else at the party was wandering
back and forth, but she had headed straight toward her
husband. She had looked at him warningly, then had
taken his glass and drunk its contents herself.

Was the drink full? Voelker had asked. Or had Sloane
already had some of it?

Snooky strained his eyes upward in an effort to
remember.

He couldn't say for sure. He thought the glass was
pretty full. Sloane might have had a few sips. Laura seemed
determined to catch him before he had any more.

Well, that was one for Sloane's story, thought Voelker.
Although it was still very weak, in his opinion. Sloane was
a rich man now and didn't have a domineering wife to deal
with. Murders had been committed for a great deal less.

But there was still the minor question of proof. It had
happened at a party, in a room full of people, any of whom
had more than enough opportunity to slip something into
a drink. No one had seen anything, really. Not that he had
expected anyone would. People at a party were not usually in their most observant state.

He checked his list. Two more people to go. Freda
Simms. Best friend of the deceased. And her boyfriend,
Eddie Bloom. He looked at his watch and thought, I can
interview both of them and still be home in time for
dinner.

The interview with Eddie Bloom was short and to the
point. Eddie was a short, slight man with shiny dark hair
and the face of an intelligent rodent. He said he had met
those people only once or twice before. He was sorry
about the lady, but he didn't know anything. Freda would
know. Yes, he had met her about a month ago, and
frankly, he didn't know her all that well either. She had

gotten drunk last night and he had driven her home. That was it. He didn't think he'd be seeing too much of her. She was upset over her friend's death, and upset women gave him a queasy stomach. He had a nervous stomach, Eddie did. He was a sensitive person and had to protect himself.

Driving away, Voelker thought two things. One was that he believed Eddie when he said he knew nothing concerning Laura Sloane's death. The other was that Eddie was a miserable little weasel.

Freda was still in shock. During the course of the afternoon, she had been to the hospital, then to the Sloanes' house, then back to her place, then to the Sloanes' again. She had been comforting Isabel when what's-his-name, her young friend, had arrived. Freda had tactfully gotten out of their way. Although they acted more like brother and sister than anything else, she had had time to notice. She had also seen Walter while she was at the house. He looked so awful . . . just awful. Like his world was collapsing. Of course the one thing she had to say about Walter was that he had always loved Laura. You couldn't help but love Laura. Laura was . . .

But that wasn't the point. What was the point, Officer?

That nice man Detective Voelker said gently that he would like to talk about the party.

"Oh, the party," said Freda. She lit a cigarette. "I don't know. Am I wandering? You must forgive me. I really don't know what I'm saying. What do you want to know about the party?"

Had she seen anything unusual, he wanted to know. Anything out of the ordinary.

"Well," said Freda, "there was something a little strange."

What was that?

"It was something that didn't happen, rather than something that happened."

Detective Voelker looked politely inquiring.

"It was Walter and Harry." Freda gave a weary cackle, a faint echo of her usual robust laugh. "They're always at each other's throats. Over the stupidest things, really. Like water resources in the Amazon, or something. I can't keep track of it myself. But last night—nothing! No argument—nothing! I keep thinking of that, and wondering why. That old ass Harry was driveling on as usual about something, Beethoven, I think it was, and Walter didn't say a word. Well, I ask you, why not?"

The last two words were said almost belligerently.

Voelker did not reply, and after a moment Freda said, "Maybe it was because he didn't know anything about Beethoven. That's possible. But it seemed significant, somehow."

Voelker nodded solemnly and wrote down, *Wandering. Drunk? Unreliable witness.*

Freda had not seen much else. She admitted candidly that she had been more than a little drunk. She smiled briefly when Voelker mentioned the name of her companion of the night before.

"He's a clown," she said. "A professional clown. I like unusual men."

Yes, thought Voelker. You would. He looked at her hair, its unnatural color, and at the lines on her face. Inwardly he grimaced.

"Laura was my best friend," Freda was saying tiredly. "My best friend. We went everywhere, did everything. Traveled. Laura was fun, she was *alive*, she—" She shrugged. "What can I say? It's a loss, Officer . . . a great loss . . ."

Voelker asked whether she had seen Laura take the drink from her husband's hand.

Freda didn't think so. No, she hadn't. She hadn't paid much attention to old Wally. Not that she ever did. Last night she had been trying to see that Eddie had a decent time.

"Yes," said Voelker politely. "Yes, I see."

Freda looked up with a sudden flash of interest. "You mean it's possible the—the poison was meant for Wally?"

Voelker debated what he should say. "Mr. Sloane himself advocates that point of view," he said carefully.

Freda stared at him, her mouth open. Then she began to laugh. She laughed and laughed and laughed.

Then, just as suddenly, succumbing to the liquor she had been drinking all day, she began to cry. She cried and cried, her shoulders heaving.

Voelker watched this performance with interest. Was it a performance? He didn't know the woman well enough to decide.

"Poor Laura," Freda gasped at last, fingers fumbling on the table for her drink. "Poor Laura. Somebody tried to kill that bastard, and *she* dies instead!"

3

"Pretty weak story," said Philip West. He had been listening carefully to Voelker's report. "Pretty weak story. Don't you think?"

"Sloane's?"

"Yes."

"I agree."

Philip West was chief of detectives in the Ridgewood Police Department, and most of the people who worked for him tended to agree when he delivered himself of a judgment. He was a big barrel-chested man with a rumbling laugh and intelligent gray eyes. He narrowed his gaze on Voelker and said, "Somebody slipped poison into his glass and his wife just happened to take it away from him? Doesn't sound too likely."

"No. On the other hand—" Voelker paused.

"What?"

"Well, it's not the kind of story you'd think up beforehand. Not polished enough. If you were going to kill your wife, wouldn't you come up with a better alibi?"

"I wouldn't know," Philip West said dryly. "What about this Sloane? Is he smart or stupid?"

"Smart."

"Hmmph. You think it might just be true, what he's saying?"

"Maybe."

"You have somebody who says he saw Mrs. Sloane take a drink out of her husband's hand?"

"Yes."

"Hmmpph."

There was a long silence. Then: "What else are you following up on?"

"The insecticide didn't come from the Sloanes' house. They have a garden shed all right, but they only have rose spray and it's the wrong kind. Of course, if Sloane did it, he could have disposed of the bottle already. So could anyone else. But we're looking. It's an unusual kind of insecticide. Might not be too hard to trace."

"Anything else?"

"I've talked to everyone who was at the party."

"And?"

"Nothing much yet," said Voelker guardedly. West might be his boss, but he liked to keep some of his thoughts and intuitions to himself.

West grinned. "No one broke down and confessed, eh?"

"Not exactly."

"Keep on it," West advised. "You might get lucky."

The funeral was held three days later. Everyone came. Freda Simms had dyed her hair black, in mourning, and was dressed in black from head to foot, with not a piece of jewelry to relieve the somberness; "very unlike her," whispered Heather to Ruth. Freda loved jewelry and usually wore an inappropriate amount of it. Today she was a still, subdued little figure, the black outfit diminishing her in size. She cried all throughout the service.

Everyone drove out to the cemetery and stood huddled close together under umbrellas as Laura Sloane's casket was lowered into its grave. It was early May, wet and dreary, a day with all the colors washed out of it. The cemetery seemed to go on forever, and Snooky found the sight of endless rows of tombstones marching over the hills on either side of them unbearably depressing. Everyone wept; everyone except for Isabel, Richard and Snooky, who stood a little apart from the others. The minister said a few touching words and it was all over. They filed silently back to their cars, the men mutely slapping Wal-

ter Sloane on the back, the women giving Isabel a hug. No
one seemed to know what to do. There was supposed to
be a little reception afterward at the Sloane house, but it
was obvious that no one wanted to come. The memory of
the party last Saturday night still lingered. Sam and Ruth
Abrams murmured excuses and drifted off. So did Heather
and Harry Crandall. Freda Simms did not even bother to
give an excuse; she simply got in her scarlet Jaguar and
drove away, gunning the engine as she went.

When Snooky got home from the funeral, he sat in the
living room with his sister and described how everyone
had behaved.

"Freda Simms looked like she was headed for a nervous breakdown," he told Maya, who listened intently.
"That gray-haired woman, what's her name—Ruth Abrams—
looked confused, as if she had just come from another
planet. Nobody knew what to say to the family afterward."

"You are the world's worst gossip," said Maya. "Go
on."

"That professor, Harry Crandall, looked as if he wanted
to shove the minister aside and give his own sermon. You
know the type. His wife looks like a hippie from the
sixties. Really. Long brown hair parted in the middle. I
went up to her afterward to make sure her necklace wasn't
a peace sign."

Bernard sat quietly in the background, drinking coffee
and glancing through the newspaper. When Snooky paused
for breath he said abruptly, "Who cried?"

"Well—nearly everyone, Bernard."

"Everyone?"

"Well, Isabel didn't. Maybe just a little. She's not that
way. Not very emotional."

Bernard lapsed back into his habitual silence. After a
while he stretched, picked up his coffee cup and left the
room.

Maya watched him go. "It's so unlike Bernard," she
whispered. "I've never known him to be so interested in
people he didn't even know."

"Well, frankly, Maya, I've never known him to be

interested in people he did know. Me, for instance. I don't feel he's interested enough in me."

"Snooky, you never feel *anyone* is interested enough in you."

They were still discussing the murder a little while later when Bernard drifted back in.

"There's no more coffee," he said.

Maya gave him a reproving glance. "Bernard," she said, "what are you going here? Shouldn't you be working on that new book?"

"Yes."

"What's this one called?"

"I haven't decided yet."

"What's it going to be about?"

"I don't know."

"Sounds like it's going fine," said Snooky. "Listen, Maya, I'd still like to invite Isabel over to dinner sometime. Is that okay? Do you think she'll come?"

"Sure. Why wouldn't she?"

"Oh, I don't know. We were never very close in college. And then with all this stuff happening to her, I'm not even sure she wants to see me again."

"I've never heard you sound so insecure," said Maya severely. "Buck up. Go call the woman and ask her."

Snooky got up and restlessly skimmed his fingers over the bookshelves.

"Look at this. Your wedding album. You've never showed it to me."

"For good reason."

"Why?" He took it down and opened it. "You had a wonderful wedding. You did it in style. Bridesmaids, a caterer, champagne fountains, the works. And William in a corner, crying as he made out the checks. It was a perfect day."

"Bernard, stop him," said Maya. "If he sees those pictures he'll never let us live it down."

It was too late.

"Look at this," said Snooky, gawking. "Geez, I had forgotten. Six bridesmaids all in purple. Six groomsmen in tuxedos. Here's Bernard in a tux. You look just awful, Bernard. A little jittery, eh?"

"I do not look awful."

"Terrible. Just terrible. And here's Maya." Snooky paused wickedly. "You look beautiful, Maya. Don't be ashamed. No, really. That gown was worth every penny it cost the family."

"Drop dead, Snooky."

"And here's William, looking like he's at a funeral. Is that his checkbook he's clutching to his heart? And there's Emily, the old bitch, looking sour as ever. And their little brats." Snooky was not a model uncle. "And here I am, looking like a total jerk. Note that I do not spare myself in my criticisms. I never did look good in a tux."

"You looked fine. Put that thing away now."

"Tell me, Snooky," said Bernard. "What do you think your wedding will be like?"

"Oh, I'm planning to get married in Las Vegas by an Elvis impersonator. They have ministers there who double as Elvis impersonators. That's just one reason why Las Vegas is the cultural capital of the world."

"Go call your friend," Maya said. "You can invite her for dinner tomorrow, if you want."

"Thanks, My."

Snooky left the room. Bernard picked up the wedding album. He and Maya leafed silently through the pages.

"Oh my God," Maya said heavily. "Look at *that*. Bernard, we must have been out of our minds. Why in the world didn't we elope? Look at your cousin there. God, she looks awful. What kind of pose is that? What were we thinking of?"

"William does look like he's at a funeral," said Bernard. "I never noticed that before."

"Why are your mother's eyes closed in all the family group shots?"

"Why does Snooky look like he's in a great deal of pain?"

"What is your cousin doing with that dog? Oh, God, why did we keep this thing? Put it back before it gets me crazy."

There was a silence. Maya said musingly, "I suppose Snooky will be getting married someday. Hopefully not someday soon, but still . . . Bernard, do you have that tuxedo, or did we store it somewhere and lose it?"

"I think it's in the guest-room closet."

"Good. Maybe if the moths haven't eaten it, you can wear it to Snooky's wedding. How does that sound?"

"I'm not wearing a tuxedo in front of any Elvis impersonator," Bernard said with feeling.

Ruth Abrams and Heather Crandall were discussing the murder over cups of grain coffee at Heather's kitchen table. It was a gorgeous spring day; the sun streamed in and the room was light and cheerful. The windows were open and the green and yellow curtains swayed in the breeze. Ruth was wearing an old cotton dress with a faded floral print; her hair was ruffled and untidy. Heather managed to look neat and self-possessed, as always, in an embroidered caftan. Her hair was smoothly plaited into a long brown braid that hung down her back.

"Nobody would want to kill Laura," Ruth was saying with conviction. "*Nobody!*"

"I agree."

"It must have been some kind of accident."

"Absolutely."

"But what kind?"

"I think," said Heather, "that it comes from too much meat-eating. Meat promotes aggressive tendencies. If I've said it once, I've said it a thousand times. Vegetarianism is the way of the future."

Ruth submitted meekly to another cup of the grain coffee. She added skim milk, stirred it and wondered if there was enough coffee and cream left at home for her to have a *real* cup when she got back.

"Meat, caffeine and sugar," Heather was saying. "The deadly trio."

"Oh, yes, yes. I tried your brown rice syrup the other day," Ruth said with forced cheerfulness. "It was very good."

"Oh, did you like it?"

"Mmmm, yes."

She omitted to tell her friend that Sam had taken one

bite of the overly sweet cake and had refused to eat any more. Even the cat would not touch it.

Heather's dog, Mahler, wandered into the room and came hopefully to the table for scraps. Ruth wondered idly if Mahler was also a vegetarian, like the rest of the family. It seemed likely. She could not imagine Heather buying cans of dog food at the market. It was against everything she believed in. Ruth could imagine her friend preparing careful portions of vegetarian fare for Mahler: perhaps stewed carrots, with tofu "meatballs" (Heather's specialty) and, who knows, maybe lettuce or whole grain crumbs for texture. Poor Mahler. She gave him a surreptitious pat on the head as he stretched out under the table. He would never know the joys of a normal dog's life.

"Mommy," said a voice from under the table. Linus was playing there, unseen as usual. "Mommy."

"Yes, darling?"

"Can I sit on Mahler?"

"No, darling." Heather put on what she called her "stern face." She peaked under the table. "You know better than that, Linus. Mahler is a sentient being, like you and me. Do you like it when Charlie sits on you?"

"No."

"Well, then."

Apparently satisfied with this line of logic, Linus went back to playing with blocks or whatever he was doing under there. He was such a quiet child, Ruth thought; it was restful to have him about. Not the way her two children had been, certainly; they were grown now, but when they were young it was like having a pair of whirlwinds in the house. And her grandson, Marcia's son Melvin, was just the same.

"How's Melvin, by the way?" Heather asked, in her casually intuitive way.

Ruth shrugged. "Who knows?"

"Do you hear from Marcia?" Heather asked gently.

"Not often. Not nearly often enough, frankly. I'm worried about her," Ruth said. Her anxious face contracted into tight little lines. "Although what's new about that? I'm always worried about her."

Marcia was her 23-year-old daughter, and she was an

enigma and a mystery to her parents. At the ripe age of sixteen she had dropped out of high school and set off, as she put it, to "find her true self." Apparently her true self was living somewhere in California, because that was where she went, with a battered suitcase and a head full of empty dreams. She drifted up and down the coast, getting odd jobs, writing back enthusiastic letters about her lifestyle and the "fantastically interesting" people she was meeting. One of those fantastically interesting people was Melvin's father, whom Marcia met while she was working in a temporary position at a pizza joint. She stayed only a few weeks, then moved on—that was her rule, never too long in any one place—and a short while later found she was pregnant. Marcia was delighted. She hadn't planned it, of course; she never planned anything; but she took it in her stride. Ruth and Sam were somewhat less delighted. To this day, the only thing they knew about Melvin's father was that he had been young, around Marcia's age, and that, according to their daughter, he made "awfully good pizza."

"Hardly sterling qualifications," Ruth would say miserably. "Hardly Harvard Law School, for goodness sakes. We had hoped for—for something a little *better* for our daughter."

"It's karmic," Heather would reply. She was of a different generation than Ruth's daughter, but sometimes she talked the same way. "It's karmic, Ruth. You have to accept it. Marcia's your daughter, not your toy. You have to accept her as she is."

This was difficult for Ruth to do because she desperately wanted Marcia to be different. She wanted her to be well-educated and successful and married to a man who was the same. Instead, all she had were letters postmarked from California which detailed Marcia's wanderings up and down the coastline from small town to small town, and which included details of her jobs at a Dairy Queen in Espolito ("*really* interesting—great people, and Melvin ate like a pig"), or a little health food restaurant on the beach near San Diego ("*heavenly* epanadas, honestly, the best I've ever tasted").

"It's not *fair*," Ruth would wail. "It's not fair! Where

did she come from? She could have dropped in from
another galaxy for all I know about her. Honestly, she just
doesn't fit into the *family*."

The *family*, in Ruth's world view, consisted of Ruth,
Sam, and their son Jonathan. Jonathan was twenty-eight
years old and, in Heather's opinion, a stuck-up prig. He
had been a pale shifty child with a nervous face who had
grown up into a pale shifty young man with a nervous
face. His intellectual prowess had not counted for much
while he was growing up, and he had become used to the
cries of Nerd and Cauliflower Brain, but it had come in
surprisingly handy later when he found himself enrolled
for a doctorate in mathematics at Princeton. Jonathan was
the Abramses' idea of what their child should be. He
taught math at Princeton and had the uncomfortable habit
of staring at you palely when you asked him a question
about his work.

"Believe me," he would say scornfully, "you couldn't
possibly understand."

Ruth and Sam were very proud of him. He came home
occasionally for visits and sat around the dinner table
thinking Large Thoughts about his work. Heather had
watched Jonathan grow up, and she had always privately
considered him a difficult child. He was spoiled by his
parents and led to believe that the intellect was everything; that as long as you were smart, you didn't have to
be a good or kind or interesting person as well. Secretly
she cherished a fondness for Marcia, the outcast, the
rebel. Marcia who, when Melvin was born, imperturbably
slung him on her back and carted him along on the road
with her.

"My daughter," Ruth would confide in a nervous whis-
per, "is a—a *hobo*."

"Marcia is a lesson for you, Ruthie. Dealing with her is
meant to teach you something."

Ruth didn't know what that could be, except perhaps
the true meaning of the word "frustration."

"Maybe," she would say politely. "Maybe."

Inside she felt resentful. Heather didn't know what she
was talking about, with all this talk of karma and lessons.
Heather had Little Harry and Charlie and Linus, three

perfect children, none of whom had ever given her a day's worry in her life.

Aloud she said, "Sam can't figure Marcia out."

"It's a lesson," Heather responded sagely.

Occasionally Marcia would show up on her parents' doorstep and expect to be fed and housed for as long as she wanted. Of course they always took her in and gave her her old bedroom back and made up the guest room for Melvin. Ruth was always secretly delighted to see her. She *was* their daughter, after all! And they were always happy to spend time with their grandson, who was now five years old and a tiny demolition machine. Melvin's infrequent visits were trying times for the cat, which spent its time trying to elude Melvin's grasping hands and slink away out of sight behind the furniture. Melvin also had a habit of biting people, which Marcia did not seem to consider a negative quality in her child.

"He's uninhibited," she would explain vaguely while Melvin sank his teeth into his grandmother's leg. "I'm raising him without *restrictions*." She said the word fastidiously, as if it left a bad taste in her mouth.

"Melvin," Ruth would say, trying to disentangle her grandson from her leg. "Melvin, darling—*ow!*—Melvin, now, don't *bite* Grandma—"

Sam, his grandfather, would object to this.

"I'll give him some restrictions," he would growl. As mild-mannered as Sam was, the sight of his grandson hanging onto Ruth's leg would send his blood pressure rocketing. He would stride forward and struggle to break Melvin's leechlike hold. Once he even added a hearty wallop, which was the beginning of a fierce argument with Marcia.

"I won't have him hit," she said furiously.

"I won't have him biting your mother," Sam growled.

"I've *never* spanked him, not once."

"That's obvious."

"You think he needs a spanking, don't you?" Marcia said. "You think he needs to be spanked?"

"Yes, I do!"

"Well," said Marcia, "you spanked me when I was little, and look how *I* turned out!"

She was well aware what a disappointment she was in their eyes. This answer left her father momentarily fuddled. Marcia scooped up Melvin and vanished upstairs.

Ruth recalled unhappily how, on their last visit, Marcia and Melvin had been home for about a week when one day Sam was standing at the window looking proudly out over the lawn. Sam and Ruth lived in a small white A-frame house in one of the less affluent sections of Ridgewood. Their house had existed for thirty years in a state of slow decay: the roof caving in, the black paint on the shutters peeling, the boiler breaking down. In the back, however, was a little patch of lawn which Sam was proud of and which he tended religiously. He would mow the grass every few weeks, use pesticide on it, and reseed it every summer. This day he was gazing out the window when he noticed that, at regular intervals, the grass had been dug up and clods of earth showed moist and brown against the lush green. He was horrified.

"What is it?" he cried. "Are there *moles* in the lawn?"

It turned out that there were no moles; there was, instead, Melvin. Melvin had spent the previous day digging up parts of the lawn with one of his grandmother's treasured family sterling silver spoons. There had been a very large argument that time; an argument of great intensity and duration. Marcia had even threatened to pack up and leave. As it turned out, she *had* packed up and left a few days later—her departures were as abrupt as her arrivals—but by then things were amicable again.

"Sam could never, ever hold a grudge against his family," Ruth told Heather, thinking of Marcia's visits.

"Really?" Heather gave her an odd sideways glance. "How about someone outside his family?"

"What do you mean?"

"Well, how about Walter, for instance? I heard—you'll forgive me, Ruth, but I heard—that Walter has been trying to push Sam out of the business?"

Ruth stared at her, astonished. How did . . . how did that get about . . . how did people find out so *fast* . . . ?

"I don't know anything about that," she said with dignity. She sipped her grain coffee and looked woodenly at her friend.

"Yes, of course. I'm sorry, Ruth. I didn't mean to bring it up. I really didn't. It's just . . . it's just that we heard . . ."

Ruth's tiny reserves of dignity collapsed.

"Oh, all right, if you have to know. I suppose Freda told you?"

"Well, yes. She heard from Laura."

"Naturally." Ruth sounded bitter. "Well, the truth is that Walter *is* trying to push Sam out. After all these years, Heather . . . after all the time Sam has spent in the company. . . ."

"It's terrible," Heather said with a quick rush of sympathy. "Awful! But it's just like Walter, now, isn't it? He can't stand having someone be next in line. You know that's what it is, Ruth. He has to control everything himself."

"We've been so worried." Tears filled Ruth's mud-colored eyes. "What are we going to do? Sam can't get another job . . . not at his age . . . we've never been rich, but at least he's always had a steady income. . . ."

"I'm so sorry, Ruthie. But it may not happen. With Laura gone—Walter has so many other things on his mind. He must realize that he needs Sam now."

"You don't understand," Ruth said. Tears ran down her face. "The worst thing isn't the money. It's what—it's what it's doing to *Sam*. He's worked hard all his life . . . what it's doing to his ego, Heather, it's terrible. His self-confidence—well, it's gone—completely gone."

"And Sam is the only business partner Walter's ever been able to keep, and as a personal friend too. How long have they been together—twenty years? Twenty-five? It's awful, Ruth, I know. I don't blame you for being upset."

Ruth lapsed into incoherency. "Please, Heather. You mustn't—you mustn't—really, you *mustn't* tell anyone, all right? It's important. And especially—you know—you mustn't breathe a word to the police. That man—Detective Voelker. You won't tell him, will you? Sam and I have been frantic. It would look—it would look as if Sam were *involved,* somehow."

"Of course I won't. Don't be silly. Some more coffee?"

Ruth sniffed and glanced down at her cup. "No, thanks."

"A little peppermint tea? It's good for you, you know. Picks you right up."

"Oh, okay. Just a little."

The child's voice from under the table made them both jump.

"Mommy?"

"Goodness, Linus! What is it?"

"Can I have something to drink, too?"

"How about some papaya juice?"

Linus nodded eagerly. That was his favorite.

"All right. One peppermint tea and one papaya juice, coming right up. Are you okay, Ruthie?"

"Yes," Ruth said vaguely. "Listen, Heather. You'll do what I said? You won't tell?"

"Of course I won't," said Heather. "Now stop worrying. I know Sam would never to anything to hurt Walter—however much the old bastard deserved it!"

Once Snooky finally got up his nerve to phone her, Isabel Sloane accepted his dinner invitation eagerly.

"I need to get out of the house," she told him. "I'm sick of cooking and cleaning. Richard and Daddy can fend for themselves for once."

She hung up and went to her closet with pleasurable anticipation, looking for something to wear. The red silk . . . too fancy, maybe. How about this skirt and blouse combination? The color, a pale blue, set off her eyes. Yes, that would be nice.

She was on her way downstairs, her mind full of plans for the next evening, when she heard a commotion in the living room. There was a loud crash.

"Now look what you've done!" It was her father, and he was furious. His voice held the scathing note that always made her flinch instinctively away. "You clumsy, irresponsible—"

"It wasn't my fault!" Richard's voice was higher than usual, strained to the breaking point. "It was an accident! I didn't see it!"

"You idiot! It's priceless! A sculpture Laura brought back from the Orient!"

"It was an *accident*, Dad!"

"Jackass! Get out of my sight! But clean it up first!"

"*No!*" Richard was screaming now. "No, I won't! Leave me alone! *Leave me alone!*"

He ran out of the living room and up the stairs, brushing roughly past Isabel. His face was white and twitching. His door shut with a bang.

Isabel sighed. It was always like this. Daddy was so difficult. But usually Richard was more understanding. . . .

She went into the living room.

"Daddy—" she said.

She stopped at the threshold.

Her father was leaning over some shattered pieces of china on the floor. One of the shards was in his hands, and he was crying. Sobbing quietly to himself, his thin body bent over ludicrously.

Isabel went back into the kitchen.

So he really did love her, she was thinking, as she got out the food for dinner. *So he really did, after all* . . .

*   *   *

Bernard, who loathed company, spent the first half of dinner glowering across the table at their attractive guest. Isabel looked at him coolly, seeming to sum him up in a glance, and then proceeded to ignore him.

Maya, as Snooky had predicted, filled in the empty gaps in the conversation by telling stories about her brother as a child.

"Once when we were kids, Snooky decided he was going to build a tree house in this big oak we had out back. Well, he built it all right, and the first time the wind blew it fell down. Just sort of collapsed."

"I was in it at the time."

"You were okay. We all had a really good laugh." She smiled fondly. "Then there was the time he took the little rowboat out. It sank, of course. Hadn't been mended or patched or whatever it's called for years. We sent the dog in to rescue him."

"None of you could be bothered to do it."

"As I remember, the dog swam a lot better than you did."

"I was little. I hadn't even taken lessons yet."

"Then there was the time he locked himself accidentally in the back bedroom. William and I told him that he'd never get out, so he climbed out the window, fell two stories and broke his leg."

"Gee, I'm enjoying myself," Snooky said. "More wine, Isabel?"

Isabel was not enjoying herself. She and Maya had taken a definite dislike to each other at first sight. That Bernard hated her went without saying. She did not yet know that Bernard hated everyone. She toyed unhappily with her fork and commented on how delicious the food was.

"Thank you," said Maya. "Want some more of anything?"

No, said Isabel. No, thank you, she had had enough. She lit a cigarette and inhaled deeply.

"When I was little," she said, "my brother and I used to play a game on my parents called 'Who can get into trouble first?' It was almost always Richard, although sometimes I won. Richard was great at getting into trouble." She paused reflectively. "But whoever got caught, the other one always stood by them. We'd lie ourselves blue in the face. It used to drive my parents crazy."

"You sound like you're really close," said Snooky.

"Oh, yes, I guess we are."

"Richard's lucky," said Snooky, with a smirk at Maya. "Now, I never had a sister who would stand by me. Maya would rat on me every chance she'd get . . ."

Later, over the dirty dishes and globules of food scattered across the kitchen, Maya said sharply to her husband, "Bernard, please stop looking at her that way."

"What way?"

"Stop giving her the evil eye."

"Well, I don't like her," said Bernard with his usual honesty.

"That's not the point. You could at least be civil."

"Why? You don't like her either, My."

Maya banged two pots together in fury. "So what? At least they're just friends, whatever that means. What does that mean, Bernard? And where's that dessert, for crying out loud?"

                    *   *   *

That night in bed Maya and Bernard had a conversation.

This was not unusual for them; they often talked in bed. Bernard, so silent with others, was loquacious with Maya. He brought up subjects; he offered opinions. He had never been that way with anyone else. It was one of the reasons he had fallen in love with her.

"Bernard?"

"Yes?"

"About this girl Isabel."

"Mmmhmm?"

"I don't like her."

"I don't like her either."

"Why is Snooky trying to get so friendly with her?"

"God only knows why your brother does anything, Maya. I've certainly never been able to figure him out."

"She's very attractive."

"Snooky is not only the perennial adolescent; he's also the perennial younger brother. I'm sure that's all he is to her."

"He's liked her ever since college, Bernard. He told us so. But he doesn't know her very well. There's something— something very cold and calculating about her. I don't like it."

"I don't like it either."

Silence.

"Are you asleep?" she asked.

"No. Are you asleep?"

"No."

They lay together, staring up into darkness. Bernard rolled over and took her into his arms.

"I've been thinking a lot about this murder," he said. "It's been bothering me."

"Me, too. Bernard, do you think—do you think there's going to be another one?"

"I don't know. It depends. If somebody was trying to murder Laura Sloane—well, then obviously they can stop. But if someone was after her and her husband, or just Sloane by himself, then—"

"Then they'll try again."

"Yes. Unless all the police activity has scared them off for a while."

"I have to say I *really* don't like Snooky getting mixed up in this. He's so pigeon-brained, it's just like him. He has no danger instinct. He's so *naive*."

They cuddled together comfortably. Maya said drowsily, "It's this murder, isn't it, Bernard? That's why you haven't been working on your book."

"I have too been working on my book," he said coldly.

"Really? What's it called?"

"It's called *Mrs. Woolly Goes to Afghanistan*."

"I see."

"I plan to have her take a tour, get captured by the mountain people and made into a rug."

"Sounds educational."

"Yes. Look, Maya, if it'll make you feel better, I can have a talk with your brother tomorrow. Let him know how we feel."

"Oh, thank you, honey. You know Snooky hasn't listened to me since he was six years old. He might listen to you. Do you know, I think he's a little afraid of you."

Bernard was pleased by this. "Really?"

"Yes."

"You're just saying that."

"No, no, Bernard, you can be quite terrifying when you want to."

She gave him a loving hug. From the foot of the bed there came a low yelp, and the dog scrambled up onto the quilt. She wormed her way up to their faces and sniffed them over thoroughly. Then she snuggled down, her tongue lolling blissfully over the pillow.

Bernard leaned over to kiss his wife. "Good night, honey."

"G'night, Bernard."

"Good night, Misty," said Bernard, but the dog was already fast asleep, her stomach heaving in little whistling grunts.

4

The next day Bernard summoned Snooky into his study. Bernard and Maya had each chosen one of the spare bedrooms on the second floor as an office. Bernard's was a small room with windows looking out over the back lawn; it was lined with bookshelves and dominated by a massive cherrywood desk that Maya had found in a dusty antique store in Vermont. The desk was nearly a century old and was battle-scarred, covered with graffiti etched into the wood by previous owners: T. and J. Hopstead, June 6, 1910; Billy Inching, 1951; even, on one of the lower right-hand drawers, a little heart with *Emily and Harris* scrawled on it, no date. Bernard loved his desk. He knew every scratch and scar on it. Now he motioned to Snooky to sit down and the two of them sat and stared at each other for a while over its vast, cluttered surface.

"Well, this has been fun," Snooky said at last, breaking the silence. "Is there any reason you invited me here, Bernard?"

"Yes."

"Dare I ask what it is?"

Bernard nervously linked several paper clips together to form a chain. "Your sister is worried about you."

"That's nothing new. Maya is always worried about me."

"She's afraid you're going to be the next victim."

"Me? That's absurd. Nobody's after me."

"How do you know?"

"I just know these things, Bernard. It's like the cross-word puzzle. Whatever's going on with Isabel's group of friends has nothing to do with me."

Bernard was interested in this. "You just know?"

"That's right."

"What else do you know?"

Snooky shifted in his chair. "I notice things," he said slowly. "The way people look at other people. What they say. People tell me things, I don't know why. It's always been like that. Maya says it's because I'm basically inoffensive."

"Quite a compliment."

"Oh, Maya adores me. You know that."

"Snooky, you were at that party last week. What did you notice? What did people say to each other, how did they act?"

"Oh, Bernard. Come on. You wouldn't possibly be interested."

Bernard gave him a cold fishy glare.

"Try me," he said.

"Mom," said Little Harry, depositing his bulk on the kitchen chair, which creaked ominously.

"Yes."

"I'm hungry."

The perpetual cry of the Crandall children.

"Have a carrot."

"I don't want a carrot."

"Have some celery."

"I don't want any celery."

This interchange took place without heat on either side. It was a custom; a ritual.

Heather had a brainstorm.

"Have a raw yam."

Little Harry was intrigued. He took the well-scrubbed yam and gazed upon it. "Raw yam?"

"Good for you," said his mother. "Lots of potassium."

"Yeah? Okay."

Munching on the yam, he left the room.

A few minutes later his father walked in. He had just come from lecturing to a class at the university.

"Hello, Harry." Heather gave him a fond kiss.

"Hello." He put his briefcase on the table.

"How was your class?"

"Morons," said Harry cheerfully. "Morons, all of them. In my day, graduate students had to have a modicum of intelligence in order to get into a program. Now it seems that's no longer required. They're drones, Heather; mindless drones."

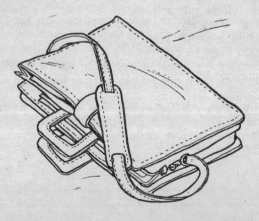

"Really? What a shame." Heather had heard this before. She briefly recalled, from her graduate student days, the general student opinion concerning Professor Crandall. "Pompous ass" and "platitudinous old fool" were two of the kinder comments. She smiled to herself. The comments had stopped abruptly when she had announced her engagement. Humming, she put aside a dish of marinated tofu and began to mince garlic, one of her least favorite tasks.

"Note-taking machines," her husband was saying with relish. "That's all they are, note-taking machines. In my day, students were encouraged to *think*. That's what education was all about! Not all these notes and memorization. The only questions I get are about the final exam next week. How long will the test be? Will it be essay or multiple choice? Basically they're asking whether they'll have to think or not. Sometimes I feel like strangling them, the whole lot of them. The academic world would be better off, I'm convinced of it."

"Yes, dear."

Dinner was prepared, served and eaten. Little Harry, full to the point of explosion, staggered into the living room. Heather poured out the tea for herself and her husband.

"Harry, I wanted to tell you something that Ruth mentioned to me."

She told him all about the conversation she had had with Ruth; all about Sam's problems with the business. Her husband listened attentively.

"Sounds like Walter," he said when she was done. "He'd stick a knife into the back of his best friend. What's Sam doing about it?"

"What *can* he do?"

"Nothing much, I suppose. Walter holds the reins. Still, they've practically been partners in that business for so many years . . ."

"I know. I don't know how Walter can live with himself. The man has no conscience at all."

"None."

"By the way, you absolutely can't tell anybody else, all right, Harry? I swore to Ruth that I wouldn't tell."

"All right. Probably everyone knows, anyway. News like that gets around."

"There's something else." Heather paused uncertainly. "I think it's too bad that nobody's gotten together since—well, since the party. It's as if everyone is afraid. So I had an idea."

She wanted to have a little get-together—"nothing elaborate, just our friends"—the following weekend. "It's about time that we got together again. It's ridiculous not to, don't you think?"

Her husband was amenable. Little Harry, when he heard about it, was delighted.

"Carob mocha brownies!" he said from where he lay on the couch.

"Yes," said Heather. "And corn chips—homemade—and veggies with dip, and cider. And apple walnut crumble."

"Hurray!" cried Little Harry.

The next day Heather called all her friends to invite them to her party.

"Ruth, you and Sam must come. This Sunday at one o'clock. *Please.*"

"Yes. Yes, of course. Naturally we'll be there. Can I bring anything?"

"No, no. It's just going to be a light lunch. Nothing fancy."

"Yes," said Ruth. "You know, Heather, since our talk, I really feel that things are going to be better. I told Sam about it. I feel—I don't know. I feel more optimistic."

"Good. Good. See you Sunday?"

"Oh, yes."

Freda sounded drunk when Heather called. Heather looked at her watch. It was three in the afternoon.

"Sunday?" Freda said, in that too-hearty tone she assumed when drunk. "One o'clock? What's the point, Heather?"

"What do you mean?"

"What's the point? Why have this party?"

"I just thought that it would be nice if everybody got together again."

"Sounds dangerous to me."

"What?"

"This particular combination of people proved fatal the last time," Freda said dryly.

"Oh, *Freda*."

"All right, all right, I'll be there. Eddie won't, though."

"No?"

"I haven't seen him since the police went round and talked to him," Freda said. She sounded almost amused. "Do you think it's something in his past?"

"Oh. I'm sorry."

"I'm not. Not at all. See you Sunday."

If Freda had seemed reluctant, Walter Sloane was downright insulting.

"Don't be such an ass, Heather," he said over the phone. "No. I'm not coming."

"But Walter, the *whole point* is that—"

"I don't care. Listen to me, Heather. One of my so-called friends tried to kill me. If you think there's any way I'm ever going to be in the same room with any of them again, you're wrong. That includes you and Harry. I don't know who did it, or why, but I'm no fool. Frankly, this invitation makes you two seem like the prime suspects."

He banged the phone down.

"Charming as always," said Heather out loud. She waited, then redialed the number.

"Walter?"

"What is it now?"

"Linus has something he wants to say to you." She handed the phone to the five-year-old and whispered in his ear.

"Uncle Wally?" said Linus. "Why aren't you coming to Mommy's party?"

Heather could not hear the reply.

"I wish you'd come," said the little boy. "Why won't you come see us?"

He listened for a minute.

"Okay. Okay, I'll tell Mommy. What? Okay. Bye, Uncle Wally."

Heather took the phone.

"Heather," rasped Walter's furious voice, "that was low. That was really low."

"Walter, it's important to me that you come to this party. It's for you, really. You and Isabel and Richard. We're not just your friends, you know. We're family. It's important that everyone not be afraid to get together again. Can't you see that?"

"I hope you're satisfied," he snarled. "I'll be there. One o'clock sharp. But I'm not *eating* anything."

He slammed down the phone and Heather sat back with a satisfied smile. She looked at her youngest child.

"Uncle Wally is angry," said Linus. "He's always angry, isn't he, Mommy?"

"Yes, dear."

Linus toddled off and she sat musing on human relationships. Here was Walter Sloane, the feared, the terrible; and he was mere putty in the hands of a five-year-old boy. It had been that way since Linus was born. He and Walter had taken to each other immediately. Linus called him Uncle Wally and sat on his knee and talked to him with the unselfconscious chatter of a child; and his doting Uncle Wally brought him presents and toys and got down on his hands and knees to play with him. No one could understand it. Walter had never been particularly close to his own children. Yet with Linus it was different. Linus expected him to be his friendly Uncle Wally, and to everyone's surprise, for the duration of each visit he was.

"That was low," Walter had told her; "really low." Well, perhaps it was. But she did want him to be at her party. Smiling, she took out a note pad and began to make a list of things she would need.

"There's a letter here for you," Maya told Snooky.

"For me?"

"Yes. It's from William."

"Oh, *hell*." Snooky picked it up gingerly. "Not another letter. How does he know I'm here? Who told him?"

"I did."

"Traitor. Foul traitor."

"He called the other day and asked me whether I knew where you were. I told him you were in my living room."

"What did he say?"

"He made a kind of strangled sound and said he was sorry to hear that."

Snooky opened the letter and read it with increasing despondency. Maya sipped her coffee and watched him.

"What does it say?"

"The usual. When will I get a job? How long do I think my share of our parents' estate will last? And so on. He says at the end that he and Emily and the kids are going to the Rocky Mountains for a vacation. Gee, I hope they have a nice time, don't you?"

"Poor William. He hasn't given up on you yet."

"You have, though, haven't you, Maya?"

"Oh, I never had any hopes for you to start with, Snooky."

"There's the telephone. Do you want to get it, or should I?"

"You get it. It'll be the only thing you've done for us the whole time you've been here."

"Hi, Isabel," Snooky said into the phone. "How are you? Yeah? Yeah? Yeah? Really? Yeah? Yeah? Okay. Yes. See you then. Really? Okay. I'll ask them. Talk to you later. Yeah. Bye."

"One of the more stimulating conversations it's ever been my pleasure to overhear," said his sister, unfolding the newspaper and squinting at the crossword puzzle. "Snook, what's a four-letter word that means 'antelope, African variety'?"

" 'Kudu.' That was Isabel. She wants to invite us to a party some friend of her father's is giving. All of us. That means you and Bernard, too."

"Oh, no." Maya glanced up. "Not *Bernard*. Bernard can't go to that party. Didn't you tell her?"

"I thought I'd ask him first."

"Well, don't say I didn't warn you. You know Bernard never goes to any parties if he can avoid it. There's absolutely zero chance of your talking him into a party given by some friend of Isabel's father. Bernard never goes outside the house unless someone's paying him."

"Agoraphobia is a terrible disease."

"He's not agoraphobic. Not at all. He's a writer, Snooky. He hates people. Especially children. My God, how he hates children."

"But he writes for children."

"Yes. Ironic, isn't it?"

"No way in hell," Bernard said later, when the idea was presented to him.

Snooky quirked an eyebrow at him. "You and my sister have been married too long. That's exactly what she said you'd say."

"Some party given by a friend of Isabel's father? You must be out of your mind," Bernard said irritably. "Go away. Leave me alone."

"Honestly, Bernard. You're so weird. You're—what's the word?—anthropophobic?"

Bernard regarded him doubtfully. "I thought that meant cannibals."

" 'Anthropophagi,' " supplied Snooky automatically. "Man-eater. Are you sure you won't come?"

"Go away and leave me alone."

"But I thought you were so interested in all these people."

Bernard put down his pencil and regarded Snooky thoughtfully. "I am."

"Then why don't you come meet them all? This is the perfect opportunity."

"I don't want to meet them," snarled Bernard. "You've met them. That's enough."

"Oh, come on."

"Go away, Snooky."

Maya came upon Snooky in the living room a short while later. He was collapsed in a chair, his long legs stretching out toward the empty fireplace.

"What is it, Snooks?"

"Oh, I was just thinking. I was trying to decide what it is I like best about Bernard. Is it his congeniality, or his tactfulness?"

"Bernard is a special kind of person. He's the kind of

person who hates everyone else on the planet. You have to understand that."

"Well, I'm going to the party anyway."

"That's fine. You can tell us all about it. Bernard and I will sit near the door with bated breath waiting for you to get home."

"I don't understand, Maya. Don't you like to go out once in a while?"

She ruffled his hair fondly. "We do go out, just the two of us, quite a lot. And Bernard may not be the most sociable person I've ever met, but being married to him has other advantages."

"Such as?"

"Such as I love him. Now shut up and stop brooding. I'd like some help with dinner, if you're not too busy."

Heather Crandall looked around her living room with a satisfied air. The party was going beautifully. It was almost as good as one of Laura's—not quite, but almost. People weren't sparkling the way they did at Laura's, but then, this was a difficult occasion. The guests were, naturally, a little subdued. Ruth and Sam were listening to Harry quite peacefully, not bothering to object or interrupt. Freda and Walter were standing *together* in the corner, conversing amiably, which must be a first, thought Heather. Isabel and Richard and Isabel's new friend, what's-his-name, were standing by the buffet table picking at the food. Heather glanced at the food and felt she had surpassed herself. It was all natural, all good, and very delicious. Little Harry had passed his judgment on it earlier, before the guests arrived.

"Great," he had declared, wolfing down the portion of food she had set aside for the kids' lunch. "Great, Mom, just fabulous. You've got nothing to worry about."

Of course she never served alcohol. She didn't approve of it, especially in the afternoon. Freda looked a little lost without a glass in her hand. Heather crossed to the buffet table and poured a hefty glass of the punch, which consisted of various natural unfiltered juices and pure sparkling seltzer. She put it in Freda's hand.

"Thanks, Heather," Freda said. She looked absolutely terrible, as if she hadn't slept for weeks. She was still dressed in solid black from head to toe.

"Punch. It's good for you. Try it."

Heather moved away, glancing back at Freda's drawn and worried face and wondering whether she should talk to her about the restorative powers of vitamins B and C, particularly the whole B-complex . . .

Walter was drinking the punch like there was no tomorrow. Heather felt pleased. Of course he considered it safe, since it was in a large glass bowl and everybody was drinking from it. Still, he seemed to like it. His glass was empty, so she took it and refilled it from the punch bowl. She could hear him talking avidly to Freda. To Heather's surprise, they were discussing Laura.

"She always loved to travel," Walter was saying sadly. "You know that picture we have over the fireplace? She brought it back from France the last time we went. She always swore it was a Watteau. It wasn't, of course, but she got a great price on it. My God, that woman could bargain."

"I remember when we were in Hong Kong, years ago," Freda replied. "Laura hit the stores there and they were never the same again. She could bargain them down to practically nothing. I remember once when she saw a ring she liked, an emerald, diamond and sapphire ring . . ."

Heather went back to the buffet table and stood there anxiously checking the food. Was everything all right? People seemed to like the cheese and crackers, but her specialty, marinated tofu, was still untouched. She took a plate and scooped some up. Well, she would show them. Was there enough punch? If not, she could send Harry out to the store . . .

Harry was having a good time. He was talking about somebody named Miltiades, an ancient Athenian statesman. Heather listened in amazed tolerance. Really, Harry was something else. Even after twenty years she was still learning things about him. Who would ever have thought that he would know anything about Athenian government?

Harry left Sam and Ruth and went over to prey upon Walter and Freda, who were deep in their reminiscences and did not even notice him. He stood there uncertainly for a moment, then joined Heather at the table.

"Good food," he said, putting an arm around her shoulders. "Good party."

"Do you think so?"

"Yes. Stop worrying. Everything's going great."

Sam and Ruth came over to talk to Walter and Freda. The men shook hands self-consciously. Ruth looked worried; but then, thought Heather, Ruth always looked worried. She was wearing a lacy pink dress whose hem was starting to unravel. Her eyes darted nervously over Walter's face as he talked.

Sam, on the other hand, seemed fairly relaxed. Whatever the problem was, he wasn't letting on. He treated Walter with an easy familiarity. Walter, on his side, seemed boisterous and in a good mood. He always was, thought Heather cynically, when he was eating and drinking at somebody else's expense.

Although he wasn't eating anything. He hadn't touched any of the food, just kept drinking from the punch bowl.

That friend of Isabel's was looking very thoughtful, Heather noticed. His eyes were on Walter. Isabel and Richard did not seem to be having a very good time. The three of them, the younger generation, stood close together and spoke very little.

Where was Linus? thought Heather suddenly, in a panic. Where was—oh. Of course. Little Harry and Charlie were out for the afternoon, but Linus had insisted on coming to the party to see his Uncle Wally. Now he was playing with blocks underneath the buffet table. She had to lift up the tablecloth to see him.

"Hi, Mommy."

"You okay?"

"Uh-huh."

"Good."

That resolved, she went to join the group around Walter. Walter had objected to something Harry said and it looked like a fight was brewing. Adroitly, Heather turned the conversation elsewhere and pressed more food on everybody.

The party lasted for another hour or so. People left in ones and twos, thanking her profusely at the door.

"Great party," Sam said, kissing her cheek. "See you soon?"

"Of course."

"It's our turn to have everybody over next," said Ruth.

"That's great," said Heather doubtfully. Ruth was a dear, but she wasn't much of a hostess or cook . . .

"Thanks so much," Ruth was saying. "I think it really helped—*really*—to get the two of them together like this," she continued in a low voice.

"Oh, good. I'm glad."

Freda left, followed by the kids—Isabel and Richard and Snooky—and Heather, with a sigh of relief, went back into the living room.

"Harry?"

She looked out onto the patio. Harry was showing Walter their garden. It wasn't much of a garden, really just a row of geraniums and a row of tulips, but Harry was inordinately proud of it. He was a fanatical gardener and spent a lot of his spare time in a pair of old overalls, rooting vengefully for weeds.

As she watched, Walter suddenly put his hand on his stomach and staggered forward.

"Heather!" Harry called. *"Heather!"*

She ran outside. Somehow they managed to get Walter inside and help him onto the sofa. He was groaning and his breath was irregular.

He muttered faintly, *"Poison . . . !"*

"Call the hospital," Harry said sharply. "Get an ambulance. I'll find that book—I have a book on poisons—"

Heather ran out of the room, her heart racing.

She dialed the hospital emergency service. Her fingers were trembling so badly she could barely push the buttons on the phone.

"Please," she said. "Please—I need an ambulance—right away—232 Glenview Road—somebody's been poisoned—"

On her way back to the living room she nearly collided with Harry running down the stairs. He was holding an old threadbare book marked *Household Poisons and Their Cures.*

"Milk," he barked at her. "Or water. Maybe milk *and* water. I haven't had time to look it up—"

"He needs to throw up," Heather said vaguely. "Or is that bad for him? My God, Harry, what are we going to *do*?"

Harry was thumbing frantically through the book.

"If only we knew what it was," he muttered. "There are so many different kinds—"

"Insecticide," Heather said firmly.

He looked up at her. "You think?"

"Insecticide. It's what—what Laura died from. Oh my God, Harry, here's the ambulance!"

In the living room, Walter was in a bad state. He was groaning, his face was white and he was in convulsions. To her astonishment, Heather found herself eyeing the lamp he had knocked over and wondering if it were broken.

She felt as if time had slowed down. She watched as if from far away as the ambulance crew rushed in and bundled Walter onto a stretcher. The next thing she knew, he was gone.

Suddenly she found herself running out of her house and screaming down the street after the departing ambulance.

"He *couldn't* have been poisoned here!" she cried idiotically. "He couldn't! It was all *health food*!"

5

Jim Voelker was back at the hospital, talking to the same young resident. His name was Dr. Winston and, if anything, he looked more tired than before. There were blue shadows under his eyes and he looked as if he would very much like to yawn but did not feel it was appropriate.

"Same poison as the wife," he was saying. "Definitely. A rare kind of insecticide. I grabbed him as soon as he came in and started the antidote procedures. Even so, it was a very close shave."

"There's no chance—" Voelker hesitated—"that he was faking it?"

The shadowed blue eyes looked at him in faint amusement.

"None at all."

"Was it a large dose? Can you tell?"

"Large enough. It's hard to gauge the exact amount, of course. Depends on body metabolism and other factors. But it was a toxic dose, all right."

"How long before he came in would you estimate the poison was administered?"

"Hard to say. The first symptoms appeared approximately twenty-five minutes before he got here, according to the report. With this stuff, he could have ingested it anywhere between an hour, maybe an hour and a half before that. It takes a while to show up."

Voelker nodded. That fit. The insecticide was slipped into Walter Sloane's glass sometime during the party.

"One more question. How long do you intend to keep him here?"

The doctor shrugged. He made a notation on the chart. "He'll be here maybe four, five days, recovering. After that, who knows? Frankly, this is one patient who doesn't want to go home. He keeps telling me that someone in his close circle of friends is trying to kill him. He doesn't feel safe outside the hospital."

The tired blue eyes looked straight at Detective Voelker.

"An attitude like that doesn't exactly help in a quick recovery. And frankly, I can't blame him. Whoever gave him that dose of insecticide wasn't trying to be friendly."

"Yes. Thank you, Doctor. You've been very helpful."

"You're welcome." Dr. Winston wandered off toward the nurses' station and, Voelker noted, the coffee machine that sat perking invitingly.

Incongruously, Voelker found himself thinking about Walter Sloane's hands—those long, fretful hands that moved and plucked nervously as he talked. What had the man done that somebody wanted to kill him—had struck twice at his family, and probably would again? For Voelker was sure that the two poisonings were done by the same person. Same method, same setting; the hallmark of a murderer. Someone in Sloane's immediate circle; perhaps in his own house. Voelker thought of the two children, Isabel and Richard. They had a better motive than anyone else to kill off their father and stepmother. Money! How many crimes had been done for money? But there was another motive that Voelker had seen many times in his professional career, and that was a secret grudge. Sometimes a grudge of long standing, one that had grown and festered silently over the years. Everyone in Sloane's circle of friends had known him at least twenty years. Except Freda Simms, of course, and she had her own reasons to hate him. He had stolen her best friend.

Voelker thought about Freda Simms. He pictured her in his mind, her blazing red hair, her world-weary expression. A jealous woman, perhaps. A possessive woman. Jealous of the things and people that belonged to her.

Could she hate Walter Sloane enough to want to kill him?

Voelker thought it was possible. He reflected also that he did not yet know enough about this case. It was interesting. He would have to talk to everyone again, everyone who had been at that party. Of course they were hiding things from him. People always did. He would just have to find out what those things were.

His final thought on the subject was that he was hungry and it was time for lunch. His list of suspects could wait. There was a little diner around the corner that served a terrific roast beef sandwich on rye with brown mustard, the good kind. He hurried out of the hospital.

Freda Simms was at another party. Her hair was blonde now—she had stripped the dark color and redyed it. *So* bad for the hair, but what could you do? She was wearing a tight shiny dress with sequins which looked very good on her. She was dancing with a friend of a friend of the brother of the hostess. None of these people knew anything about Walter or Laura or their friends, and she was glad of that.

She had not been upset to hear about Walter's near brush with the Great Beyond. Not at all. Why should she? Her only regret was that whoever had tried to kill him had managed to get to Laura first . . .

Of course she felt sorry for the kids. Nice kids, both of them. Still, if old Wally kicked the bucket, they would get all his money, which wouldn't be too bad.

Old Wally! She wondered how he felt after his close encounter with death. Frightened, probably. Scared shitless. She would be.

The man she was with smiled and swung her around in time to the beat. He was good-looking; better-looking than Eddie, and he was a terrific dancer. So was she. She smiled back and laughed; her familiar loud cackle. It pierced through even the dance music and the people around them turned and smiled.

She was having a good time—a very good time. Why the hell shouldn't she, after all? Life was short!

Life was short . . .

Old Wally should know that by now!

Bernard was grilling Snooky about the Crandalls' party. "So as far as you could tell, no one handed Sloane a drink except for Heather Crandall?"

"That's right. And maybe Isabel. She always tries to help out that way. I try to discourage her, but it's no good. She says everyone expects it."

"Who was standing next to Sloane at the party?"

"Freda Simms, for most of the time," said Snooky promptly. "Then Ruth and Sam Abrams came over. Professor Crandall tried to talk, but everyone ignored him. And of course his wife was in and out, filling everyone's glasses and trying to get them to eat that disgusting food."

"But you didn't see anything suspicious?"

"No. Nothing at all."

Bernard regarded his brother-in-law coldly. "I thought you were the observant type—the type who just 'notices things'?"

"I don't have radar, Bernard. I couldn't keep my eyes on everyone in the room the entire time."

Whoever was doing this was clever, Bernard thought. He or she hid their actions in a noisy, crowded roomful of people. Who in the world would be paying attention at a party?

They went over it again and again, but it was always the same. Basically, anyone could have done it. Anyone at the party. Snooky hadn't seen anything out of the ordinary. He had left, with Isabel and Richard, before Sloane had come down with the first symptoms.

"I see," said Bernard. He lapsed into a disapproving silence.

"I'm sorry. I wish I *had* seen something. But—"

Maya came into the room and looked fiercely at her brother. "This is ridiculous. Two parties, two murders. Starting to get the picture yet, Snooky?"

"Oh, stop fretting, My."

"I don't understand it. Why do you have to go to all these stupid parties? Why can't you and your friend go out on real dates like normal people?"

Snooky looked thoughtful. "I don't know, My. I guess it's because I haven't asked her. It's not a bad idea. Maybe going to a movie would get her mind off of things." He slouched out of the room.

"My God," said Maya, watching him go, "it's just like having a teenage son. Isn't it, Bernard?"

"Maya, let's never have children."

"All right, darling," she said absently.

"Listen, a movie isn't such a bad idea for us, either. Why don't we go out tonight, just the two of us? It would be fun, and we could get away from your brother and his weird problems."

"That's a great idea. Where's the paper? Where's the movie page? Is there anything playing around here? You know, we haven't had an evening out for a while now."

"Away from Snooky."

"Exactly."

They had their heads together over the paper and had almost chosen a movie, *Flight of the Zombie Bats*, when Snooky slouched back into the room. He looked dispirited.

"Isabel won't go," he announced mournfully. "She says she can't, she's too busy, what with visits to the hospital and taking care of her brother and all. I guess I understand."

He looked around the room. "Hey," he said brightly, "how about a movie, just the three of us?"

"I'm a *mess*," wailed Ruth Abrams over the phone. "A mess. I'm so upset over this latest thing with Walter, I can't tell you. Sam has been working twice as hard since Walter's been gone, and it's nearly killing him. And worst of all, the children are coming for the weekend."

"Marcia?" said Heather with interest.

"And Jonathan. And Melvin, of course."

"Poor Ruth. Everything happening all at once."

Ruth grew confidential. "It's getting sort of exciting, though, isn't it, Heather? I mean—I mean, *who* do you think is doing it?"

"I don't have the faintest idea. And I don't think it's exciting. Not at all. I think it's absolutely horrible."

"Oh, yes, well, yes, of course it is. Yes, of course. Naturally. Well, what I *meant* was . . ."

Of course it was horrible, Ruth reflected as she hung up the phone a little while later. First Laura, now Walter. Poisoned, both of them! And that young man who had come around—not Detective Voelker with his mournful face, another one, younger (there seemed to be hordes of detectives snooping around now)—with his polite questions about her and Sam and the business. Well, naturally she hadn't told him the whole truth. Why should she? Why should she incriminate her own husband? He had asked whether there were any problems between Walter and Sam and of course she had said no. She had given him a nasty look, too, to discourage him. She had said that Walter and Sam were the best of friends, and had been for years. They always went to each other's parties. No, she hadn't seen anyone tamper with Walter's drink. Why should she? She was minding her own business. It was so hard to believe that it could happen, anyway. Yes. It was certainly hard to believe.

And now with the children coming home for the weekend, she hardly knew what to do. She didn't exactly feel like entertaining, with all this going on . . . but children were children, no matter what their age, and you couldn't say no . . .

Sighing, she got out a recipe book and began to look up holiday meals.

"So we were wrong," Philip West said. "Somebody was trying to kill Sloane after all."

"Yes," said Voelker.

"He could have poisoned his wife," West said judiciously, "and then someone else could have used the same method to poison him."

"It's possible."

"But you don't think so, eh?"

"No," said Voelker. "I don't. I think that both these poisonings were done by the same person. The same unusual kind of insecticide was used, for one thing. I think we're looking for one person, perhaps two working together."

"Looks like it. And the motive?"

"Money is the obvious one. The Sloane children will inherit a lot of money if their father dies. In that case they must have deliberately murdered their stepmother, and then tried to kill Sloane at the party. But if the attempt that killed Laura Sloane was an accident—was really meant for her husband all along—"

"Then it's not for the money, presumably."

"No. It means that someone in Sloane's group of friends is out to get him."

"The motive there?"

"Well, everyone seems pretty much agreed that he can be a real tyrant. And Sam Abrams works with him. I'm going to have to check out their business arrangement more closely. I know that if Sloane dies, Abrams takes over."

"How about the others?"

Voelker shrugged. "Freda Simms—Heather and Harry Crandall—this young fellow that the girl is seeing—I don't know. I'll have to find out more about them."

"So let's see," said West, leaning back in his chair. "There are several possibilities. Either someone murdered Laura Sloane deliberately and then someone else tried to capitalize on the situation by poisoning her husband. Or the same person deliberately poisoned both of them. Or the murder of Laura Sloane was an accident and someone has been after Walter Sloane all along. Which is what he's been trying to tell you."

"Yes."

"In any case, the murderer may try again. He or she seems fairly determined."

"Yes."

"Motives," said West. "Motives. You have to find out more about these people."

"I intend to," replied Voelker.

Heather Crandall was not in the best of moods when Detective Voelker knocked on her door that evening. She and her husband had just returned from the Woodcrest Elementary School, where Linus was in kindergarten. They had been to see Linus's class play. It was Linus's theatrical debut and he was tremendously excited about it.

"Mommy, you *have* to come," he had said for weeks beforehand.

"Well, of course we're going to come. Your father and I wouldn't miss it for the world, Linus."

"You'll be there, won't you?" he would ask anxiously a few days later.

"Of course, sweetheart. Don't worry."

But when the time came, Heather had barely been able to drag herself there. It was only a week after their ill-fated party, and she was so depressed! To think that that terrible thing had happened in *her* house, at *her* party . . . !

She and Harry had gotten dressed up, however, and had driven with Linus and the other two boys to Woodcrest School. They had sat in the center, near the front, like good parents, quarreling with the Thompkinsons over the seats ("I believe *we* were here first," Heather said in icy tones), and applauding vigorously for all the skits. Charlie had been bored, but Little Harry was fascinated. Little Harry had not inherited his father's brains, Heather thought, watching him anxiously. He loved the skits and watched "Leaves at Play" and "Mushrooms Dancing" with an intense absorption.

They had waited eagerly for Linus's class to perform its skit, but when the time came it was a big disappointment. His class had decided to enact an invasion from outer space. Linus was one of the Earth people and had been practicing his screams around the house for days. The aliens were fitted out in old Halloween outfits, pointed ears, football helmets and the like. One of the girls, determined to be fashionable even as an alien, had convinced her mother to let her borrow her mink coat. As the aliens rushed onstage the mink coat caught on a nail on the floor. There was a loud ripping sound, followed by an even louder shriek from the center of the audience.

The aliens became confused and milled about. Several of them began to cry. Linus decided it was probably time to scream. The teacher decided the skit was over. Heather had applauded vigorously as the curtain came down, but her heart was heavy.

To her surprise, however, Linus was cheerful.

"Our play stunk, didn't it?" he said.

He had gotten a chance to scream, which was apparently all he had wanted. Heather cast him a nervous look. He was such a *quiet* boy . . . was he repressed in some way? Did he have unconscious hostility? Was he lonely? She had to admit that in spite of everything he looked the picture of emotional and physical health. He sat crammed in between his two brothers and discussed the events of the night with an unruffled calm.

Little Harry announced that he had enjoyed himself. Charlie looked disgusted. Linus spoke at length about the other two kindergarten skits and the general reaction to them. It seemed that his class's performance had been the most popular because it had been a total failure.

Heather sat back and wished that real life could only be that way!

They had barely gotten home and put Linus to bed when Voelker knocked on their door. He was terribly sorry to disturb them, but if he could just ask a few more questions . . .

"I thought we had already answered all your questions," Heather said impatiently. She was usually so beautifully mannered, but tonight had been difficult and she was tired of going over the same ground again and again.

Detective Voelker's face lengthened with remorse.

"Yes," he said. "It's difficult, isn't it? Going over the same thing so many times. Still, there are a few things we thought we ought to check—routine, you understand . . ."

They went over the party again—who had stood where, who had given Walter Sloane a drink, who was left when the first symptoms came on.

"Nobody," said Heather. "Nobody, as I've told you. Just Harry and me. Everyone else had gone already."

"Yes, yes. So you did say."

From there they turned to the past. Harry had known Walter Sloane for nearly thirty years, since Sloane had married Harry's cousin Sally. Heather had known him for twenty years.

"Who do you know who might have a grudge against him?"

Heather shook her head. "You don't understand. If this—this murderer is out to get Walter, then—well, it could be nearly *anybody*. Everybody has some kind of grudge against him. He's that kind of man. He accumulates grudges as he goes."

"What kind of grudges?"

"I wouldn't like to say," Heather said firmly. "It's not for me to implicate anyone. And besides, it's never anything serious. He just has such a bad manner about him."

Yes, thought Voelker. Walter Sloane certainly did have a bad manner about him. Still, it was not very likely that some etiquette freak was trying to kill him for that.

"Do either of you have any kind of quarrel with Mr. Sloane?"

There was no good way of asking this, so Voelker had learned long ago to state it matter-of-factly. He knew he would not get a truthful answer, but he hoped to startle them into giving something away.

All he got for his trouble was a stony stare from both Crandalls.

"Certainly *not*," said Harry with emphasis.

"You've told me yourself that you quarreled with him frequently, Professor Crandall."

"Yes, of course. Are you seriously suggesting that because we disagreed over politics or certain points of information, that I would try to poison him?"

"Of course not. Naturally not. These questions, however, have to be asked . . ."

Soon after that he found himself outside their door, on his way to the car. The atmosphere had chilled subtly after that question about possible quarrels with Sloane. Voelker found that interesting. He wondered if there was something there . . .

The trouble with these circles of friends was that they all stuck together in a primordial kind of way. We are Insiders and you are an Outsider, they said. They were so used to being loyal and keeping each other's secrets that they continued to do so, even in the face of a police investigation.

Voelker sighed. He could be missing the truth about the Crandalls. There could be nothing there. Nobody liked to have the finger of the law pointed straight at them. No one enjoyed answering questions.

That was the trouble with being the police. People had to talk to you, but they didn't have to tell you everything they knew, either!

"Bernard, why are you sitting here in the dark?"

"I'm thinking."

"Is Misty in there with you?"

A tail thumped against the floor. Maya switched the lights on.

"Honestly, Bernard. It gives me the creeps, the way you sit there without the lights on."

"It helps me think."

This was true. Bernard had conceived of the ideas for his most popular books, including the most famous of all,

Mrs. Woolly and the Bengal Tiger, while sitting in the dark.

"What, may I ask, are you thinking about?"

"Nothing."

"I see." Maya gave him a long level stare. "Well, would it disturb you if I took Misty away for her dinner?"

Misty's tail thumped harder. She jumped up from her position at Bernard's feet and followed Maya from the study.

Once they were gone, Bernard switched off the overhead light and sat in darkness for a while. Then he turned on his desk lamp and, taking out a bright green Magic Marker, began to write.

Bernard had a special shorthand system; his very own method that he had devised while working on his books. It was his firm belief that vowels were unnecessary for reading comprehension, so his system (of which he was inordinately proud) consisted almost entirely of consonants.

He said out loud, "Anomalies?" and wrote in large green letters at the top of the page,

ANMLYS?

He sat and pondered that for a while.

Then he murmured, "Jealousy," and carefully printed

JLSY

Underneath he wrote,

$$

His hand continued down the page, making sparse, abbreviated notes. . . .

"You don't understand," Isabel said the next day. "I don't *want* my father to come home."

"Why not?" asked Snooky.

"I don't like the way he treats Richard, for one thing. And I'm not happy about how he acts toward me, either. Give me a hand here, will you, Snooky?"

He unfolded the blanket she gave him and put it on the bed. Isabel was getting her father's room ready for his return.

She fluffed up a pillow, opened the window to let fresh air in and, looking around the room, said, "Well, at least he won't find too much to criticize here."

"I don't understand. You're rich, aren't you? Why don't you hire someone to help with the housework instead of doing it all yourself?"

"I'm not rich. *Laura* was rich. She was loaded. But Richard and I never saw much of it. Besides, Daddy thought we shouldn't be spoiled. Ever since I came home from college I've taken care of everybody. Laura never did, that's for sure. That wasn't her style."

She finished her inspection of the room and went downstairs to the kitchen, where she motioned Snooky to a seat at the table and brought out two cups of coffee.

"Milk?"

"Yes, thanks."

"Sugar?"

"Yes."

She watched as he put four heaping teaspoons of sugar into his cup.

"Snooky. That's *disgusting*."

"Thanks."

"You never used to drink it that way."

"What can I say?"

She lit a cigarette and smoked thoughtfully. Snooky glanced around the room. The kitchen was ultramodern, all glass and steel and shiny black surfaces. "What's with this furniture?" he asked.

"What do you mean?"

He gestured. "The walls. The chairs. The stove. Whose taste is it?"

Isabel looked around vaguely, as if seeing the room for the first time. "Oh. Laura's, of course. She did the whole house over when we moved in, after they got married. It was old-fashioned, she said, so she redid everything."

"I'll say. Is this a table? It looks like it's about to blast off."

Isabel shrugged. "That was Laura. It had to be something different to please her."

There was a pause. Snooky stirred his coffee, then said, "Listen, Isabel. Why don't you get a job?"

She laughed. "A job? You mean, to get out of the house?"

"That's right."

Isabel sighed. "Ever since I graduated, everybody I know—my father, my father's friends, my friends, everyone—has been trying to get me to go out and find a job. A *job*!" She said the word as if it offended her. "Why should I work? I like my life here, Snooky. I like sleeping late and not having to go to an office in the morning. I like having my own hours, staying up as late as I want. Nobody understands that I'm enjoying myself."

"Really? You don't seem to be enjoying yourself."

"Richard needs looking after," said Isabel, looking past him, "and of course Daddy, once he comes home again. I'm needed here." She glanced at him angrily. "Anyway, how dare you? You're the last person in the world to tell me to go out and get a job. Look at you! Even in college your brother had despaired of you. Remember those letters he used to write?"

"In college? William was writing me letters even back then?"

"Uh-huh."

"But I hadn't done anything *wrong* back then."

"He had big plans for you, Snooky. He wanted you to become a businessman or a lawyer."

"Yes. You're right. You do have a good memory, Isabel."

"You never told him your major was 'Undefined Arts and Leisure.'"

Snooky smiled. "That's right. That's what I used to call it. Of course I told William I was majoring in economics."

"It was a long time ago, Snooky."

"Yes. Yes, it certainly was."

He glanced at her. Isabel looked private, withdrawn; closed in upon herself like a spiral seashell, swirling endlessly away into the depths. Even in repose her face looked troubled.

"Mr. Sloane," Detective Voelker said, struggling to keep his temper. "Mr. Sloane, I'm just trying to do my job."

"Not very well," barked Walter Sloane. He leaned back in the hospital bed and closed his eyes. "I asked for some kind of protection after the first attempt on my life. Do I have to *die* before the police will get involved?"

Voelker viewed the long, gaunt body in the bed with active distaste. Sloane did not look well. He had been in the hospital nearly a week, but there was still a green tinge to his skin and his face was set in long anxious lines.

"I'm worried, man," he said. "Worried?—I'm frightened! Somebody's out to get me, and I don't have the faintest idea who it is. Except that it's one of my closest friends, that's for sure. Damn them all!"

Voelker had regained control of himself and now sat impassively. He had come here for a specific reason. In his researches into this case he had run up against one fact he found extremely interesting. But while he was here he was going to get as much information as he could.

He said, "Mr. Sloane, does anyone have a quarrel with you that you know about?"

"No, damn you. If I knew, would I be so worried?"

Sloane closed his eyes again. When he spoke, minutes later, his voice had changed. It was calmer, more controlled.

"I'm sorry. Damn it, I'm sorry. It's just that I've been so sick and so frightened. I knew people hated me, but I never knew—well, I guess I never realized how much."

Voelker pounced on this.

"People hated you? Who is that?"

"Everyone," said Walter Sloane. He turned his face toward Voelker and the detective was shocked to see how ravaged it was. "Everyone does. I know that. Everyone except—except Laura. And Isabel."

"Yes," said Voelker politely, and waited.

After a moment Sloane said: "Specifics?"

"Please, Mr. Sloane. It's the only way we can guarantee your safety. You must realize that this person, whoever he or she is, will try again. And you may not be the only one in danger. Your son and daughter may be also."

"Yes. Yes, I realize that."

Sloane leaned back. "Well, there's the Abramses. Ruth resents me because my marriage to Laura lifted me and my kids above them economically. Ruth and Sam are always scraping to get by."

"Why is that? Isn't Mr. Abrams more or less the junior partner in your firm?"

"Yes, but most firms have good years and bad. This last year has been bad. Thanks to Laura, I didn't suffer; I don't really need the money. But the Abramses do. And so Sam started trying to take over my job."

"In what way?"

"He started getting pushy, that's all. He wanted my job, I'm telling you. There's more money in it for him, more prestige. It made me mad. I let him know I wouldn't stand for it. He claimed the idea never even occurred to him. Damned liar. I know ambition when I see it. I'm ambitious enough myself, damn it."

Yes, thought Voelker.

Sloane shifted and turned his gaze to the window. He said unexpectedly:

"Maybe I was wrong. Going through something like this . . . it changes you. Changes your perspective on things. Maybe Sam was just trying to be helpful. Maybe he was getting grabby because it was a bad year, and he would have been all right once things settled down. I don't know. I really don't. You'll have to ask Sam and Ruth about it yourself."

"I intend to."

"I'm sure you do, you clever bastard." Sloane's voice was amused. "Don't think I don't know what's going on behind that long face of yours. Useful sort of face to have in your business, isn't it? Don't like me much, do you? Well, join the club."

Unexpectedly, Voelker found himself thawing. Heather Crandall had been right; Walter Sloane had an unfortunate manner; but he also had a kind of rough-edged charm to him. It was this, Voelker suspected, that had kept his friends around him all these years.

"Heather and Harry Crandall," Walter Sloane was saying. "I don't know. Harry's the greatest pompous ass that ever walked the earth, of course—sometimes when I hear him going on about those damned slime molds I want to strangle him—these academics, they're all alike! Idiots, all of them. Think they know better than everybody about everything. Harry was talking about Boccherini at our party, just shooting his mouth off the way he always does, even though the damned fool doesn't know a thing about Boccherini. He didn't even get the right *decade*, for Christ's sake. And as for his other theories—!"

He let the sentence linger meaningfully in the air.

"The man's a stuffed shirt. Impossible. Just impossible. Still, you know, we've been friends for a long time. I don't know why, honest to God I don't. He's Sally's cousin, of course. My first wife. They were really her friends. Everyone liked Sally. But when she died, they were stuck with me."

"Your first wife died of . . . ?"

"Cancer," Sloane said. His face collapsed as he said it. "Ate her up alive. Awful. Awful to watch. My poor dear Sally. Sweetest woman who ever lived. She was different from Laura, you know. Very different. She would listen to what I said. She was a good listener, Sally. Laura was more fun, but Sally was a better listener."

"So you don't know anything against the Crandalls."

"Heather and Harry? What a pair!" Sloane gave a sudden loud bark of laughter. "Health food and stuffed shirt! No, I don't have anything on them, I'm afraid. Can't see why either of them would want to do me in now."

"I understand that you and Professor Crandall have had some—ummhm—loud disagreements in the past, most recently—" he consulted his notes—"two weeks before the party in your home?"

The cool blue eyes looked at him in amusement.

"I'm no fool, Detective. Don't take me for a fool. Yes, Harry and I got into a little spat about something—can't even remember—he was going on about some novelist, Danish, I think . . ." He brooded. "Pontoppidan," he said at last in triumph. "Henrik Pontoppidan. Some damned Danish novelist. Harry was blithering on about his works and I told him to shut up and play tennis. I thought he was going to hit me. Came at me with his tennis racket raised. It was his serve, too," he added musingly. "Damned fool. Going on about somebody named Pontoppidan when he should have been serving. The man's impossible. Holds up the whole game."

He glanced at Voelker again with wry amusement.

"But don't start telling me that your theory is that old Harry went home, brooded for a while and then put insecticide in my drink. Oh, no. You don't know Harry, that's all. He'd write a scientific treatise on it first. He'd entitle it 'Wrongs Suffered at the Hands of Walter Sloane,' and he'd have an index, three chapters and a summary." He roared with laughter. "That's how these damned academics handle things. Don't tell me you don't know *that*, Detective."

Voelker leaned forward. This was what he had come for.

"Mr. Sloane. *Where do you think your money would go if you and your family all died?*"

Sloane stared at him in surprise.

"I don't know. I've never thought about it. My whole family? I can't say."

"Besides your children, you don't have any living relatives, do you, Mr. Sloane?"

"No. No, I don't." Sloane mused for a moment. "I was an only child."

"No aunts, uncles, cousins?"

"No."

Voelker nodded. That was what he had come up with in his research into Sloane's past. He said slowly, "Do you think it's possible—just possible—*that your money might go to the Crandalls?*"

Sloane stared, shook his head, laughed.

"What are you suggesting, Detective? You're crazy! Harry and Heather? You mean you really think they're planning to kill off all four of us for the money? Assuming they would even get it, which I doubt. Don't be idiotic. I'm sure the idea has never even occurred to them."

Voelker did not reply.

"You mean you think Heather plans to poison us with her damned carob brownies or damned sparkling punch, eh? No, no, no. You've got it all wrong."

"I would like to point out, however, that they are your only living relatives, Mr. Sloane, even if their relationship to you is through marriage."

Sloane grew reflective. "Yes, I guess they are, although I must say I've never thought of them that way. Sally's cousins. Yes, I guess they are."

There was a silence. Voelker said, "That brings us to Mrs. Simms."

Sloane shook his head. "Freda hates me," he said. "No ifs, ands, or buts about it. The woman hates my guts."

"Why is that?"

"Laura," Walter Sloane said simply. "Freda was Laura's best friend in the world. When Laura and I fell in love and got married, Freda nearly went to pieces. She couldn't share her, you see. She hated me on sight. Jealous woman. She had rages—awful. Laura would cry for days after talking to her. But she eventually settled down. We would socialize, you know. It was never comfortable, of course, but . . ." He shrugged.

"How do you feel about her, Mr. Sloane?"

"Freda? I don't like her. Never did. Thought her rages and jealousy were absolutely ridiculous. I told Laura repeatedly to drop her, but of course she wouldn't hear of it."

"So Mrs. Simms definitely dislikes you."

"I should say so, yes."

"Enough to try to poison you?"

There was a long silence.

"Could be. Could be. It's possible. Freda was always trying to get Laura to travel with her, the way they used to in the old days, before our marriage. It upset Laura to say no, again and again. They had a scene about it—oh, not too long ago."

"When?"

"Let me see. Oh, about a month before our party. It took Freda that long to cool off. The woman has a temper, I'll tell you that. She and Laura had just made it up and were friends again in time for the party."

He sighed. "I don't like Freda, but I can't believe she'd be a murderer. Although if she was going to murder anyone, she'd certainly start with me." He gave another loud yelp of laughter. "The old bitch!"

But it was said almost fondly. He closed his eyes.

"I'm tired," he said. "Tired. Is there anything more?"

"I'm sorry, Mr. Sloane. Just a few more minutes of your time, if I may. I wanted to ask you about the other guests at the party."

"Who was that?" He opened his eyes.

"Your children. Isabel and Richard."

"Oh! My kids! Don't be a fool, Detective. Do you really think they'd try to murder me?"

Voelker maintained a cautious silence.

Sloane lifted himself up on one elbow.

"I suppose you think they deliberately poisoned Laura, and now they're after me, the two of them, for the money? Laura's money? Don't be a fool. I tell you, I know my kids. We may not always get along, but they wouldn't try to murder me."

"Have there been any problems between you and your children, Mr. Sloane?"

"No," said Walter Sloane. "No problems. Just the usual stuff, you know, little spats, nothing out of the ordinary. Everybody has them. Go talk to Ruth about her kids, now *she's* got a problem. Not me. They're Sally's kids, Detective—good kids."

"So there haven't been any—long-term difficulties between you?"

"Listen to me," Walter Sloane said. He was sitting upright now. "I won't hear anything against my kids, do you hear? They're not killers. They're not out to get me or my wife or anyone else. So shut your big fat mouth and do your best to figure out who is!"

Which, Voelker reflected later as he left the hospital, was very definitely the end of the interview.

6

There was a scream from the den and Ruth Abrams, startled, dropped a spoonful of ice cream into her lap.

"Marcia, *darling*," she said.

Her daughter, busily knitting, did not even look up.

"It's just Melvin and Jonathan," she said. "Playing their usual games."

There was another scream, a blood-curdling scream from Melvin's childish lungs.

"What—what are they doing?" Ruth ventured to ask.

Marcia spread out the scarf she was making and gazed at it in satisfaction.

"I don't know," she said. "I don't like to ask. Probably Jonathan has Melvin in some kind of primitive wrestling hold. All I know is that Melvin loves it. Jonathan loves it too. He can pin Melvin every time."

Given that Jonathan was twenty-eight and Melvin was five, Ruth certainly hoped that was true. She mopped the ice cream off her dress with a napkin and began to clear away the dessert dishes.

Her son, daughter and grandson had descended on the house like locusts a few days ago and showed no signs of departing. Father-daughter relations were tense, with Melvin the point of controversy. Sam felt his grandson should be going to school soon. Marcia, while conceding the general point, felt that he was not ready.

"He can go in a couple of years," she said carelessly.

"He should be in kindergarten already. Linus is in kindergarten, and he loves it."

"Linus is Linus. Melvin is Melvin."

There was no arguing with this kind of logic, so Sam just watched helplessly as Marcia played with her son, who seemed more out of control on this visit than on previous ones. The cat was having an episode of hysterical fugue and had not been seen for several days, although its food disappeared when left out overnight. So far Melvin had destroyed a vase, a cookie jar, several knickknacks and an expensive glass coffee table. Ruth was looking very worn-down and oppressed. The only people who seemed to be enjoying themselves were Marcia and Jonathan, who were getting along better than they had in the past, when their respective lifestyles had diverged so drastically. Jonathan seemed to genuinely enjoy playing with his nephew, and he and Marcia had had some good heart-to-heart talks, locked away upstairs in what used to be Jonathan's bedroom. Ruth wondered vaguely what it was they talked about. Their parents, probably. Jonathan was twenty-eight and Marcia was twenty-three, but complaints about parental mistakes, miscalculations and misunderstandings never seemed to go out of style.

Jonathan appeared in the dining room, carrying Melvin upside down.

"What a guy," he said. He released his nephew, setting him carefully upright. Melvin looked around and, seeing something move behind the sofa, streaked toward it hopefully.

Jonathan was looking well, thought Ruth. His thin sallow face was lit up with exertion, and his black hair was ruffled.

"Some wrestler you have there," he said to Marcia.

"Oh, yes, he loves to wrestle."

"He'll be a big guy someday."

"I hope so. His father was."

Ruth listened from the kitchen, intrigued as always by these small revelations about Melvin's father. Marcia rarely talked about him. It was as if he had never existed.

"Have Mom and Dad told you about the double murders in the neighborhood?"

"The what?" Marcia looked up, her knitting needles poised.

"The double murders. Go on, Dad. Tell her. It's been in the papers and everything."

"Oh, Jonathan, stop it," Ruth said, bustling back into the room. "We don't want to talk about it, do we, Sam? Especially not now, with all the family together."

"Dad's taken over for Walter Sloane until he's better," Jonathan said. "Hasn't Dad told you all about it? He called me in Princeton."

"I never get any family news," Marcia said. "Everyone thinks California is too far away for a phone call."

"Well, first Laura Sloane was poisoned at one of her own parties. You remember her, don't you, Marce? Big daredevil kind of woman with a bossy manner?"

"No," said Marcia.

"Well, she's only been around here for a couple of years," said Jonathan. "I guess you didn't meet her. Anyway, first she was poisoned, then her husband was."

"At the *same party*?" Marcia sounded scandalized.

"No. Later. At the Crandalls' place."

"Oh."

Marcia seemed to feel that was all right. She settled back into her chair and picked up her knitting again.

"But he didn't die. So while he's recuperating, Dad's taken over as the senior partner in the business. Haven't you, Dad?"

"Yes," said Sam.

Ruth looked over at him proudly. And he was doing an excellent job, too. He had stepped into Walter's position without any trouble at all. It was a shame how it had happened, of course . . . it was awful . . . but then, Sam seemed to be enjoying his work so much more, and the responsibility had been good for him. He flourished on it. And the new salary helped so much in little ways. She could buy so many things that before she would have just thought about. She smiled at him proudly and said, "Some coffee, Sam?"

"Yes, thanks."

The discussion lingered on the double tragedy at the Sloanes', then turned to other topics. Jonathan was having trouble with another member of the Princeton mathematics department. Ruth gathered vaguely that the trouble centered around this other person's delusion that she was the Big Brain of the department, perhaps of the world. This infuriated Jonathan.

"The woman hasn't done any decent work in her life," he said irritably. "She's fiddled around with a little topology and differential geometry, that's all. It's crap—complete crap—child's play! Anyone could have done it. But she sits there in the departmental meetings in front of Professor Hirsch and preens herself and acts like a big shot. It *kills* me, I'm telling you. It just kills me."

Ruth understood that Jonathan was the one who wanted to act like a big shot and this woman, whoever she was, was crowding him out. She meekly continued clearing away the dishes.

Marcia said sweetly, "It takes many lifetimes to evolve past the bad karma of jealousy, Jonathan."

"Don't give me that Buddhist crap. I'm telling you, the woman's a fake, a complete charlatan."

Ruth left them squabbling about it—nothing ever changes, she thought; the topics were more mature but here they were squabbling just the way they used to when they were kids—and went into the kitchen. She was up to her elbows in soapy water, humming happily to herself, when her husband joined her.

"It's building to a crescendo out there," he said. "Thought I'd take refuge while I could."

"What are they saying now?"

"Marcia just called Jonathan a pighead, and Jonathan called her a mousy little ratface. Then she started to cry."

"Oh, *dear*." Ruth wiped her hands on a dish towel. She felt disturbed. Really, it was *just like* when they were ten and five . . . "And they were getting along so well, too," she said in despair.

"Well, it had to break sometime. Can I help?" he said, looking at the pile of dirty dishes.

"No, Sam, just stay here and talk to me. How's everything at work?"

He beamed at her. "Fine. Just fine. I've had a chance to try some new ideas that've been on my mind—oh, for years now. And they're working out great, Ruth. I'm happy about it, I really am. Everyone else seems to be pleased, too."

"Oh, *good*."

"You know, it's so different when Walter's there. He keeps everybody in order, sure, but he's so tyrannical. Constantly flying into one of his rages and screaming at everybody. Everyone hates it. With him away, the office is just so peaceful."

"Oh, I'm glad."

"And frankly, Ruth, I'm enjoying the new position. Lots more responsibility, and I don't have to kowtow to anybody. It's great. I'm enjoying myself."

"Oh, Sam," his wife said happily, "I knew you would. I always knew you would."

Something in her tone made him look at her sharply. She was not watching him; her head was bent over the sinkful of dishes.

"Oh, yes," she went on airily, "I always knew you'd love it!"

*   *   *

"Phone call for you," said Maya, appearing at the door of Bernard's study. "It's Mrs. Crandall. You know. The one who gave that party."

Bernard looked surprised. "Why is she calling me?"

"She wants to talk to you about your books. She's a big fan, she says."

"Which books? The rat ones?"

"No." Maya glanced at him uneasily. "I think it's—you know—Mrs. Woolly."

"Good Lord, no. Not Mrs. Woolly. Maya, *please*."

"I already told her you were in. I'm sorry, Bernard."

He followed her into their bedroom and reluctantly picked up the phone.

"Hello?"

"Oh, Mr. Woodruff, this is truly a pleasure. My name is Heather Crandall, and I'm such a fan of your books, I've read them to all my children—well, actually, not all of them, Little Harry is too old, but Charlie, when he was younger, and now Linus is such a fan!" She ended on a thrilled squeak. "And I just learned from Isabel that her friend is actually your brother-in-law! Isn't that *something*?"

Bernard remained impassively silent.

"Well, *anyway*," said Heather, plunging on, "I know it's a great favor to ask, and it's probably a big intrusion, but I was wondering if I could bring Linus by to meet you? And perhaps you could autograph a copy of his most favorite book of all, *Mrs. Woolly Goes to Market*? It would be such a thrill for him, he's only five years old but I've read all your books to him—"

"No."

There was a startled silence. "Excuse me?"

"No. I'm sorry, Mrs. Crandall. I don't let people come to my house. I don't sign autographs, and I don't like children. Good night."

He hung up, to meet Maya's frozen glare.

"Bernard, you are terrible. You are a terrible human being, do you know that? The poor woman just wants her child to meet an author—"

"I hate Mrs. Woolly," said Bernard. He went into his study and closed the door.

"Now that's interesting. That's really interesting." Voelker nodded approvingly at his subordinate, detective Rick Connors.

"I thought you'd think so, sir." Connors was his junior in years and experience, and always deferred to him very gratifyingly. Voelker, who knew the scope of Connors's ambitions, was not deceived.

"Two glasses with his fingerprints on them," mused Voelker. "Both glasses also had Mrs. Crandall's prints—and one had Mrs. Abrams's as well?"

"Yes, sir. Badly smudged, but they were there."

"And only the one with Mrs. Abrams's prints had poison in it?"

"Yes, sir."

Voelker pondered this. Why *two* glasses? Heather Crandall had been serving everyone at the party. Perhaps she had switched the glasses inadvertently, or—

Or perhaps she had deliberately tried to throw suspicion on her friend, Ruth Abrams?

Voelker considered Ruth Abrams. So vague, so muddleheaded—could she really have planned these crimes? Well, of course you never knew. It seemed unlikely, but . . . Heather Crandall had been serving everyone from the punch bowl, so naturally her prints would be on all the glasses. It made a convenient excuse for her. But now he knew that Ruth Abrams's fingerprints were on the same glass that had contained the poison. It was odd . . . it was very odd.

It had taken a while to get permission to fingerprint everyone at the party. They had raised a squawk, of course—always did, these people—but in the end everyone had submitted. They all felt insulted at being considered suspects for murder. That professor, Harry Crandall, had gone all red and talked about calling his lawyer and about his constitutional rights, until his wife had calmed him down. But they got the fingerprints in the end. Funny.

The Abrams woman hadn't complained at all, just sat meekly during the process. Perhaps she didn't realize . . .

She wasn't very intelligent.

It had looked bad for the Crandalls before this—having the man poisoned at their house, during their party. But now with this new evidence . . .

Of course, he realized that if the Crandalls had poisoned their friend, they wouldn't have left the glass lying around where the police could find it. They would have been sure to wash everything up and put it away quite innocently. Instead, when Voelker arrived there, they had acted their parts very convincingly. Heather had been in tears, ranting something about her food, and her husband had been standing by her side, looking shattered and lost. Dishes and utensils and napkins and glasses were scattered about, just as they were at the end of any party, apparently undisturbed. Voelker had instructed that the food, the punch bowl, the glasses, *everything*, be taken away and analyzed.

Voelker did not smile. He never smiled. But inside he felt a growing sense of excitement. Before this—just gossip, innuendo, suspicion flying about. Nothing concrete, nothing definite. Now at last they had *something*. It was inconclusive, of course. There was no saying that the person who had slipped poison into Sloane's drink had even touched the glass. Still, it was something.

He shuffled the papers in front of him and said to Connors,

"Let's go have another talk with Mrs. Crandall."

Heather was polite but definite.

"No, of course not," she said, shaking her head. "I'm sure I didn't switch anyone's glasses during the party. I went to the punch bowl, filled it up and came back. How could I switch glasses? No, I'm quite sure, Officer."

"Did you at any time see Mrs. Abrams handle Mr. Sloane's glass?"

Heather's gaze became frozen. "No. No, I didn't," she said. "No one was helping me—no one at all."

That could be a lie or it could not, thought Voelker wearily. It was impossible to tell . . .

"*My* fingerprints?"

Ruth Abrams stared, frightened, into the eyes of Detective Voelker.

"Yes, Mrs. Abrams. Your fingerprints were found on the glass which poisoned Mr. Sloane."

"But—but . . ."

Words seemed to fail her. She looked around blindly and her husband took her hand.

"That's *impossible*," said Ruth Abrams.

"I'm afraid it's true," said Voelker. "Please, Mrs. Abrams. I just want to ask you some questions. Did you at any time handle Mr. Sloane's glass?"

"No . . . no, I don't think so . . ."

"Are you sure?"

Ruth fumbled nervously with the hem of her skirt. Her husband handed her a tissue and she wiped her eyes hastily.

"I'm sorry," she said. "This is so . . . so *sudden* . . . let me think. No. No. I never once handled Walter's glass. Why should I? Heather was handing punch all around. No, I never touched it."

Voelker looked at her steadily. Next to him, Detective Connors was scribbling in a notebook.

"Are you sure of that?"

"If my wife says she's sure, gentlemen," Sam put in coldly, "then she's sure."

"I never touched it," Ruth said firmly, with a kind of dignity. "Never!"

She stood up and, swaying as if drunk, marched out of the room without asking for anyone's permission. The three men sat in embarrassed silence. After a minute the door opened and Marcia peeked in.

"Dad?" she said. "Mom's crying in the kitchen, and Melvin just bit the cat."

* * *

Later that afternoon Ruth recovered sufficiently to pick up the phone.

"Oh, Heather . . . Heather," she sobbed, losing all self-control once she heard her friend's voice.

"Ruthie? What is it? What's wrong?"

Ruth told her—about Voelker's visit, about the finger-prints on the glass. Walter's glass! How could it be?

"Heather—*they think I did it!*"

"Ruth. Don't panic. They've been here, too. My fin-gerprints were all over every single one of the glasses. They told me so."

"But—but you were *serving*."

"It doesn't matter." Heather sounded suddenly very tired. "It doesn't matter. They still *think* things. Of course they do."

"It's just ridiculous," fumed Ruth. "Absurd!"

"Well, of course it is. The important thing is not to panic. Remember that, Ruthie. Just don't panic."

"Yes . . . yes . . ."

"They asked me whether you had handed Walter some punch during the party," Heather said. "I told them no. I don't remember anyone else helping me serve. You didn't, did you, Ruthie darling?"

"Certainly not," said Ruth Abrams.

Bernard and Snooky were closeted together in Ber-nard's study. Snooky was saying, "Isabel ran into Mrs. Crandall at the grocery store. She said Mrs. Crandall told her all about it. Honestly, if you hang around that store you eventually hear everything. The other day I was there and I heard this guy near the vegetable section talking about—"

"Snooky."

"Yes?"

"Get to the point."

Bernard sat silently as Snooky told him about the fingerprint discovery. When he was finished, Bernard said:

"Interesting."

"Isn't it?"

"Very."

"I thought so, too."

Bernard mused for a moment. "Is she that stupid?"

"Who?"

"Mrs. Abrams."

"You mean, to leave her fingerprints on the glass?"

"Yes."

Snooky considered this. "I don't know. I don't think she's as stupid as everyone makes her out to be, if you want my personal opinion."

"Hmmhmm. Interesting."

"Yes."

"However," said Bernard with real regret, "I have work to do. So if you don't mind—?"

"I'm leaving. And Bernard—"

"Yes?"

"You're very welcome," said Snooky.

"I won't have chicken gumbo soup AGAIN!"

There was the sound of dishes shattering against the wall, and an angry cry from Richard.

"But, Dad, they said that you should—"

"I don't care what the damned doctor said! I want food, I tell you—real food! I want a nice juicy steak! Now bring it to me, and bring it quick, damn you!"

Isabel ran up the stairs.

"Daddy—" she said, entering the sickroom.

Her father glowered at her from the bed. "I won't have it!" he said. "No more chicken gumbo soup! I'd rather die than eat that stuff again!"

Richard muttered something and brushed past Isabel out of the room.

"Now, Daddy," Isabel said in her most consoling manner. "Really, there's no need to shout and break everything in sight, is there? All you have to do is ask. If you want a steak, then you'll get one."

Walter Sloane regarded his daughter suspiciously. "Really?"

"Of course. If you want one so badly, then your stomach must be ready to handle one. Who cares what the doctor says?"

"That's right," he muttered, leaning back against the pillows. "Damned right. Who cares what the damned doctor says? You're a smart girl, Isabel," he added approvingly. "You understand me, don't you?"

"That's right, Dad. Now just sit tight and don't go anywhere, okay? I'll bring your dinner up as soon as it's ready." She twinkled at him and left the room.

"*Go* anywhere," said Walter Sloane to himself. "As if that's likely, in my condition!"

Nothing at all wrong with him, Isabel was thinking as she went downstairs. Nothing wrong with him at all. He's just enjoying playing the invalid. He loves his sickroom and having Richard and me wait on him hand and foot.

She felt the familiar surge of resentment.

She went into the kitchen and took a steak out of the freezer. She stood looking at it doubtfully. Could you cook a frozen steak without defrosting it first?

Richard came in. "Hi."

"Hi."

"He threw the dishes at the wall," Richard said. "Soup and everything. It must be a mess. I guess I should go upstairs and clean it up."

"Oh, I'll get it later."

"No, I can't have you doing everything. Even though you're the only one he can stand. How do you handle him so well, Isabel?"

She was still looking at the steak with its layer of frost on the plastic wrapping. "What?" she said vaguely.

"How in the world do you handle him so well? I can't be with him for three minutes before I want to strangle him myself."

"Oh, I don't know. Practice, I guess. I'm a lot older than you, you know."

Richard shrugged, going out with the mop and bucket.

"I wish—" he said, his voice floating back into the kitchen, "I *wish* he had never come home!"

Isabel turned the package over in a vain search for directions. Perhaps if she put the heat up *really high* . . . ?

*   *   *

"He won't see anyone but Richard and me," she told Snooky later on the phone. "I don't know how he's going to go back to work. He doesn't trust anyone."

"That's a shame, you know, because he had such a kindly personality before all this happened. Has that detective been around to see you again?"

"No. He was here right after Daddy went into the hospital, but I haven't seen him since. I don't know what the police are doing."

"It's a strange business, Isabel."

"Yes."

They were silent for a moment. Then Isabel said, "How about a drive in the country this weekend? I'm not doing anything on Saturday."

"A drive? You mean, just the two of us?"

"Yes, of course just the two of us. What did you think?"

"I thought," said Snooky, "that I was never going to get to see you except in the company of your father's friends."

Freda Simms was seated on the couch in what she liked to call her "living area," a huge room with a marble fireplace, a spiral staircase leading up to the second floor and elegant Persian rugs everywhere. There was a bay window with a magnificent view of the lawn and trees beyond. The garden was in full bloom and she stared at it absently, nursing the drink at her side.

Some of the shrubs had been clipped into the most ridiculous shapes, *really* . . . unicorns and gargoyles and over there was one that looked just like a donkey . . . she'd have to talk to the gardener, Mr. Hal, about it. His name was Harold Shrimpton, Hal for short, but for some reason he insisted on being called Mr. Hal, like a hairdresser. She humored him. He was a very good gardener, except when his fancies got away with him. . . .

She tore her gaze away from the ill-fated shrubbery and tried to concentrate. Yes, now, where was she? Something had been bothering her for a while now, and she had finally decided to sit down and think it through. Although it wasn't really something that could be thought about or chewed over . . . it was a memory . . . a fleeting memory, obscured by alcohol and heightened hormones. She had seen something at the first party, the one at the Sloanes' house.

She sighed impatiently and shook her head. Now *what* in the world was it? It was about an hour or so before the end of the party. She had been sitting down (as she consumed more and more liquid refreshment, it became harder to stay vertical) and smiling at what's-his-name, Eddie, as he leaned over her. He had said something amusing, or at least at the time she had thought it was amusing. She was laughing and her eyes strayed over his shoulder.

And she had seen something . . .

She screwed up her face into a comical frown and sipped her drink. Something had been bothering her, moving restlessly and fretfully at the edge of her consciousness, since then. What was it?

Outside the big bay window Mr. Hal moved slowly into view, carrying a huge pair of hedge clippers. He began to snip at a previously unmolested bush. He snipped and snipped and snipped, stepping back now and then to see how his handicraft was proceeding.

When he was done, he regarded his work with quiet satisfaction. The hedge, formerly a dull boxlike shape, now resembled one of the Great Pyramids of Egypt. Its four triangular sides were as smooth as stone.

Mr. Hal smiled to himself. Behind him, in the house, Freda watched without the internal comment so often provoked by Mr. Hal's artistic efforts. She did not see the new pyramid in her garden. Her eyes blindly looked inward, backward in time . . .

Now what *was* it she had seen?

7

Bernard stared suspiciously at the little boy a few feet away.

"Who are you?"

"I'm Linus."

"What are you doing here?"

"I don't know," the boy said truthfully.

Maya entered the study, followed by Heather Crandall. "Bernard, this is Mrs. Crandall and her son Linus. I invited them over to meet you."

"Oh, Mr. Woodruff, this is such a great pleasure," enthused Heather. "I brought over some cookies for you and your wife—I hope you don't mind—and here are Linus's Mrs. Woolly books. You see how much he likes them."

Bernard glanced down at the dog-eared, much-abused copies of his books.

"I suppose you'd like me to sign them," he said dully.

"Well, yes, if it's not too much trouble. See, Linus, this is what a famous author looks like!"

Linus was not impressed. He was kneeling on the floor, trying to get Misty to wake up.

Bernard scratched his name hastily, with *To Linus*, in each of the books and gave them back.

"Thanks so much," said Heather.

"You're welcome. Now, if you don't mind, I'm working . . ."

"Heather and I are going into the kitchen," Maya interposed. "Linus can stay here with you for a while. It'll be good for him to see what a famous author looks like while he's working."

Before Bernard could protest, the two women were gone. He was alone in the room with Linus.

A stark terror filled him. It was not so much that he hated children, as he often claimed; it was that they frightened him. He did not know what to say or do. He was silent enough around adults; with children he was positively tongue-tied.

In the kitchen, Heather said, "Are you sure it's all right if Linus stays in there with him? Perhaps your husband would like to work."

"Oh, no, it's good for Bernard. He writes for children, but so rarely gets to actually meet any."

"Linus really enjoys his books."

"Well, that's good to hear. You mustn't mind his manner, Mrs. Crandall. Bernard can be a little brusque sometimes. He doesn't mean anything by it."

Snooky came in and, after saying hello to Heather, turned to his sister and sank onto his knees.

"Are you asking me to marry you?" said Maya.

"Please, Maya." He took her hand. "I have something important—very important—to ask you. I am hoping that the presence of Mrs. Crandall will make you think twice before saying no."

"Go ahead."

"Can I have the car on Saturday?"

"No."

"Please?"

"No."

"Pretty please?"

"No."

"Okay. Thanks anyway." Snooky rose to his feet and opened the refrigerator door. "What's there to eat?"

"Don't eat now. It's almost dinnertime. You'll ruin your appetite."

"I could never ruin *my* appetite, Maya. Put a crimp in it, maybe, but never any lasting damage."

"You're taking this awfully well, Snooks. What's the hidden agenda?"

"I simply don't consider your refusal as definite. I intend to try again later, repeatedly, until you change your mind, as you inevitably will, worn down in the face of my determination and charm."

"Good plan," said Maya.

"Thanks."

"Can I ask what's going on Saturday?"

"I'm taking Isabel out for a drive in the country."

"I see."

"Hard to do without a car, Maya."

"Yes."

Snooky closed the fridge door and wandered out of the kitchen. Heather said, "Your brother doesn't have a car?"

"My brother rents everything: houses, cars, everything. He has one ironclad rule: he never buys anything he can rent, and he never rents anything he can borrow. This has seen him through life so far."

"I was worried when Little Harry got his learner's permit," said Heather. "I was afraid there would be arguments over the car. But he so rarely drives it. He prefers to jog."

Back in the study, there had been a long, long silence. Linus played with Misty's ears while the dog slept, and Bernard stared mournfully at a picture on the far wall.

Finally Linus said:

"We have a dog."

"How nice for you."

Linus could not hear the sarcasm. "His name is Mahler."

"Mahler?"

"Yes."

"Oh."

That seemed to be the end of the conversation. Linus got up and came over to lean in a familiar way on Bernard's knee.

"Are you working yet?" he asked, looking up into his face.

"No. Not yet."

"Will you be working soon?"

"I don't know. It all depends."

"On what?"

ON HOW SOON I CAN BE ALONE! screamed Bernard's mind. But all he said was:

"It's hard to work. I don't do very much of it."

Linus nodded. His mind seemed to be elsewhere. He said:

"What's your dog's name?"

"Misty."

"Misty," said Linus thoughtfully. He said:

"My dog is bigger than your dog."

Bernard's hackles rose at this. How right he was never to trust a child.

"Misty is a fine-looking dog," he said defensively. "Just the right size, if you ask me."

"I don't know," said Linus, surveying her critically. "She has funny-looking ears."

"What's wrong with her ears?"

"They're all sort of floppy and everything."

"That's because she's sleeping. When she's awake they stand up."

Linus looked doubtful. "When she's awake they stand up?"

"Yes. Just like your ears. See? When you're awake they're like this, and when you're asleep they fold down and go all floppy. Like Misty's ears."

"They do not."

"Oh, yes they do."

Linus clapped his hands over his ears. "They do not!"

"They go all floppy, and collapse on your pillow," said Bernard.

Linus stared at him, his eyes wide in horror.

"They do not!"

"Yes, they do."

"Like Misty's?"

"*Worse* than Misty's."

There was a long, lingering, trembling pause. Then:

"*MOMMY!*" shrieked Linus and ran from the room. Bernard could hear him screaming all the way down the hall.

Bernard sat back slowly in his chair. Misty woke up,

scratched herself, yawned and came to rub her head against his leg.

He scratched her ears, which were floppy asleep and floppy awake. She rubbed her head and yawned in deep satisfaction.

Bernard smiled.

"I've never been so humiliated in my life," fretted Maya as Heather's car pulled rapidly out of the driveway. "Never! Honestly, Bernard, I leave the boy with you for two minutes, and the next thing I know he's in the kitchen screaming and sobbing and babbling something idiotic about his ears. I thought his mother was going to hit me."

"Children are naturally gullible."

"Children are your livelihood, and you'd better remember it. Why doesn't your publisher send you on a book tour, and you can terrify children all over the country?"

"I don't want to go on a book tour. I just want to be left in peace."

Maya sighed in exasperation. "Fine. In that case, I'll leave you in peace. That's the last time I ever invite any fans over to meet you."

"That's too bad," said Bernard to her retreating back.

"Oh, Snooky," Isabel said, "this is really beautiful."

She was gazing out the car window as the countryside flashed past. Snooky had headed due west, crossing from Connecticut into New York, then south on the Taconic State Parkway. After a short drive he had gotten off the parkway and now he turned onto a long narrow bridge over a reservoir. On either side of the car the water stretched out in a smooth shining circle hemmed in by lush green forest. There was no one else to be seen.

"Yes, isn't it nice?" he said. "It'd better be. I don't remember exactly what it was I had to promise Maya for this car, but it had something to do with my share of the estate."

"It's breathtaking. I had no idea it was so beautiful here. Oh, Snooky, look—more birds!"

Flocks of them were whirling and weaving in the dark-blue summer sky. The combination of the bright water below and the shimmering sky above made Isabel close her eyes for a moment. When she opened them, they had left the reservoir behind and were following a narrow curving path through the forest.

"Here we are," said Snooky a quarter of an hour later. He pulled into the entrance of the state park. They followed the road for half a mile until a lake opened up on one side, ringed by picnic benches. Snooky and Isabel got out of the car and stretched their legs. To their right was a small sign marked NATURE TRAIL, with an arrow indicating a dirt path that disappeared into the trees by the water's edge.

"First things first," said Snooky. "Let's eat."

Isabel had brought a large picnic hamper containing chicken sandwiches, tuna salad, green and black olives, rye bread, Port Salut cheese, coffee in a bright yellow thermos and a big chocolate cake covered with thick frosting and chocolate curls. Snooky had brought along a paper

bag containing two apples and a handful of discouraged-looking French fries.

"That's it?" she said, surveying his contribution.

"I'm sorry. It was all I could steal from the fridge. Maya was cooking dinner and she was already pretty mad about the car."

They sat down at the picnic table and ate the sandwiches. Then they took a blanket from the trunk of the car, spread it on the grass by the lake, and lay down in the sun. Snooky was busy cramming a large piece of chocolate cake into his mouth. A growing number of flies and water-insects buzzed around his head.

"How's Richard?" he asked indistinctly.

"Richard? Oh, he's difficult. Very difficult. He roars around in his car all day and takes out girls at night. I'm worried about him."

"Oh, yes. A teenage boy driving around, seeing lots of girls. That *is* cause for alarm."

"It's not just that. It's him and Daddy. They can't seem to get along at all. Of course things were never great between them before, but now . . ."

"I take it your father's not exactly the happy invalid."

Isabel launched into a long tirade against her father. Richard had a right to be angry, she said. Daddy was being impossible. He was so demanding, so difficult. He was just a big baby . . .

Snooky listened silently, brushing the flies away from his head.

Finally Isabel paused in her invective and looked thoughtfully at the young man stretched out next to her.

"You know what, Snooky? You're a good listener."

"Oh, come on."

"No, I mean it. It's a rare trait in men."

"Come on, Isabel. That can't be true. Maya says I never listen to her about anything. She tells me that a lot, in fact." He gazed absently over the lake. "I never hear her anymore."

"More cake?" said Isabel. "There's still some left."

"No, not right now." He got to his feet and brushed off the crumbs. "Let's try the nature trail, okay?"

The afternoon passed quickly. After taking the trail encircling the lake, they sat back down again on the blanket and talked quietly. Isabel dozed for a while, her head against Snooky's shoulder. There was no sound except for the faint humming of a bumblebee. Snooky watched the rippled shadows of minnows darting back and forth in the water.

Finally, as the tree shadows lengthened over the lake, they reluctantly packed up the picnic basket and set off in the car. On the way home they were both rather subdued. Now and then Snooky stole a glance at the young woman next to him. Isabel's face was calm and composed; her eyes glittered turquoise in the late afternoon light.

It was a long drive back to Ridgewood. When Snooky drove up in front of the Sloane house, Isabel gave him an odd sideways glance. "Thank you, Snooky. It's been a lovely day."

"Yes, hasn't it?"

"We'll have to do it again."

"Okay, well, fine," he mumbled, suddenly shy. "Good night."

"Good night."

She sat in the twilight, smiling at him, her blonde hair shining like a halo around her face. He did not say anything. Finally, sliding over on the seat, she linked her arms around his neck and kissed him.

After that she didn't leave the car for a long time. . . .

Maya was in the kitchen when Snooky opened the front door and drifted down the hallway.

"Hello, little one," she greeted him. "In here. Want some cocoa?"

"Okay."

"I'm making some for Bernard. He gets crazy if he doesn't have his hot chocolate at night."

"Bernard is too weird." Snooky sat down at the kitchen counter and smiled mysteriously to himself.

"What is it?" asked Maya with the wisdom born of experience.

"What is what?"

"What's happened? You look funny."

"What do you mean, funny?"

"I mean funny. Sort of googly-eyed and very pleased with yourself. Oh, *no*," said Maya in alarm. "Not you and that—that *tramp*?"

Snooky was offended and said so in very definite terms. "She's not a tramp. She's a wonderful person and—"

"Don't say it, Snookers. Please don't say it."

"What? She's a wonderful person and I think I'm in love."

He drifted away with his cup of cocoa.

"Oh, *damn*," Maya said, and bore off Bernard's cocoa to his study.

"Snooky's in love," she told him.

"What?" said Bernard. "With someone besides himself?"

"With Isabel."

"Oh, *God*."

They sat together miserably.

"It's hard, being a parent," said Maya.

It was late Saturday night and Freda was out drinking herself silly at a bar. She had always had a drinking problem—in her lucid moments she admitted that to herself—but ever since Laura had died she had been drinking uncontrollably. Morning, noon and night. She signaled to the bartender for more of the same and smiled at her companion, whose name, rather tediously, had turned out to be Freddie. It was a curse, these rhyming names—Eddie, Freddie, Teddy—how she longed for a good solid Larry or Frank.

However, "Freda and Freddie" sounded sort of cute together, she thought. She toyed with her drink and smiled at him.

"What did you say you do for a living?"

Freddie was a doctor. A doctor! That would make a change from the circus clowns and deep-sea fishermen she had been dating recently. Something solid. Something respectable. Her eyes glinted. How Heather and Ruth would talk!

Freda knew how her crowd—well, it wasn't really *her* crowd, it was Laura's crowd, and now frankly it wasn't either of theirs anymore—had felt about her assortment of boyfriends. Even Ruth, barely scraping by on Sam's salary, had put on airs when confronted with someone whom she felt was beneath her class. Freda laughed silently to herself. Beneath her class! What a joke!

But a *doctor*, now . . .

It turned out that Freddie practiced internal medicine. He had a flourishing private practice, but he was lonely. He was divorced, with two kids, both teenagers, both difficult. Freda listened while his troubles began to unfold. That was her one redeeming trait; she had always been a good listener.

Now she nodded and drank and nodded some more and drank some more, while Freddie, his face flushed with self-pity, told her the story of his life. Becoming a doctor had not solved all his problems, as he had expected it would. He was vehement on this point. It *should* have solved all his problems, but it hadn't, and now he was somewhat at a loss. His kids were both turning out to be real trouble, and they were in college at the same time and in addition he had to support his ex-wife, who showed no inclination to go out and get a job to support herself. Freddie felt that was unfair. He felt many things were unfair. . . .

The music was loud in the bar and some of his words were drowned out, but it didn't really matter. Freda nodded sympathetically and ordered another drink. Before she could touch it, however, Freddie snatched it away from her.

"I'm sorry," he said. He was a nice man; she could see that in his eyes. "I'm a doctor. I think you've had enough."

Freda looked down at the whiskey-and-soda she had ordered and thought, *But I wanted that drink* . . .

And then froze suddenly as the memory came back to her complete in every detail—the memory that she had been trying to recall for so long now . . .

She was laughing over Eddie's shoulder. Behind Eddie stood Walter, a whiskey-and-soda in his hand. As Freda watched, Laura came and snatched it away from him with a warning look, one of her famous *Don't you give me any trouble* looks—

But not before—

Not before Freda saw who had put the poison in that drink. . . .

"Freda?" It was her companion. His face was troubled. "You all right?"

"Yes." She mumbled something, pushed herself off the barstool and said rather incoherently, "Don't go—don't go—I'll be right back."

She fled for the phone booth.

Naturally the phone would be out of order. She tried it impatiently, once, twice, jangling the hook, but it made no difference. Damn it! She swung the door open and pushed her way through the crowded bar toward the exit.

Once out in the street she glanced around quickly. There was a row of phone booths over on the other side.

She swung the glass door closed and forced the coin in. She dialed quickly, with trembling hands. She found she was shaking all over; trembling with the shock of discovery and the sudden nausea she felt. *She knew who had killed Laura* . . .

The phone rang twice before it was picked up.

"Hello?"

"Hello," said Freda and suddenly, helplessly, began to cry. She sobbed for a few moments into the receiver; then flung herself against the side of the booth and wept uncontrollably.

"Who is this?" the voice on the phone was saying, "who is this?"

"It's me," she said venomously, through her tears; "Freda."

"Freda? What is it? What's the matter?"

Freda held the phone very close to her face, cupping her left hand around the receiver. She said quietly:

"*I saw you do it*. I saw you murder Laura. I was watching—I didn't know I was until just now—I just realized—*you murderer!*"

There was silence on the other end.

Freda began to hiccup. She felt acutely nauseous.

"I saw—you do it—" she said between hiccups, "and I'm going to—make sure—everybody knows!"

She was shaking violently now.

"God damn you!" she screamed into the phone.

"Freda—" the voice said in a conciliatory tone. She hung up and leaned against the booth, breathing deeply.

Nausea overwhelmed her and she staggered out into the bushes. There, with the helpless childish feeling this always gave her, she threw up everything she had consumed that evening. She thought this might make her feel better, but it didn't. She was in shock.

And now she felt thirsty. Terribly thirsty.

She went back into the bar and, sitting down beside Freddie, proceeded with determination to drink herself silly.

Freddie brought her home around one o'clock in the morning. He had found her address in her wallet and, draping her over the front seat, he drove her home slowly and cautiously. In spite of his warning she had consumed far too much alcohol at the bar, and now she could barely stand up. She fell sound asleep in his car, her head lolling back, her bright flame-colored hair spilling onto his shoulder.

She managed to get out the house keys herself. Once safely in her own living room she collapsed on the sofa and went promptly to sleep. Freddie, who was in fact a nice man, made sure she was comfortable and shook his head over her for a bit. She seemed like a decent person, he thought. She certainly was a good listener. She had listened sympathetically to his stories right up until the time when she had passed out. Freddie didn't meet very many good listeners in his life.

He shook his head one more time and let himself out, making sure the door locked securely behind him.

Freda awoke with a sense of panic. Where was she? What had happened—?

She fumbled for the light and turned it on.

Oh. Her living room. She must have gotten home, somehow. Yes. She had a vague memory of that nice man, Freddie, helping her through the door—

Good Lord, how her head hurt! And her stomach. She still felt nauseous. And confused . . .

Where was Freddie? Had he left?

The door bell rang again and she turned her head slowly. Yes. That must have been what woke her up. The door bell.

She got up painfully and moved uncertainly toward the door. Perhaps it was Freddie, coming back. Perhaps he had forgotten something, or had decided to spend the night with her . . .

Her pace quickened.

"Freddie?" she said, opening the door.

8

The scene repeated itself with the inevitability of history.

The phone rang. Ruth Abrams muttered, "Twelve ounces of chocolate, or eighteen?" and cursed mildly to herself. She was trying out a new recipe Heather had given her—of course she had made a few substitutions, chocolate and sugar instead of carob and honey, that kind of thing—and it was, as usual, not going well. She was elbow deep in cookie dough and had confectioner's sugar all over her arms and face. Her hair, already silvery, was further frosted with flour. Reaching over, she managed to locate the phone behind the mixing bowl and the recipe file.

"Ruth?" It was Heather, sounding distraught. "Ruth? Is that you?"

"Of course it's me," Ruth said irritably.

"Something terrible has happened!"

"What?" Ruth asked vaguely. Were those—were those actually *roaches* she saw at the bottom of the flour canister . . . ?

"Ruth, it's Freda. She's been killed—strangled!"

"What?"

"Strangled. Freda. In her *home!*"

"But—but that's terrible," Ruth said. "Terrible!"

"I just got a call from Isabel. She's hysterical, poor thing."

"Yes . . . yes."

"Ruth? Are you all right?"

"I just can't take it in," Ruth said, sounding bewildered. "Laura . . . then Walter . . . then Freda. It's all so—so *unsuburban*."

"Yes," said Heather, thinking how *like* Ruth it was to come out with a comment like that at this time. "Yes, indeed. I know what you mean. It's unbelievable that it could be happening here, among our friends."

A new idea had occurred to Ruth.

"I suppose this means that awful policeman will be back."

"Isabel says that the police are at Freda's house right now, looking for clues and examining the—the—"

"The body."

"Yes. She was strangled last night. Late last night. Oh, Ruth!"

"If the policeman comes here," Ruth said, "at least I'll have some cookies ready for him."

"Cookies?"

"Chocolate chip cookies."

Poor Ruthie, Heather thought. She was having a hard time dealing with all this. She had never been good at handling strain. "Call me tonight," she said and hung up.

"Yes," said Ruth to the empty phone line. She put the receiver back and wiped her sticky hands on her apron. She rubbed her face absently, leaving a smear of cookie dough across her cheek, and surveyed her kitchen in its state of disarray.

Well, that was just awful about Freda!

Not that she had ever liked her much.

She wondered if she had sounded appropriately—*regretful* on the phone? It was always so hard to know what to do or say . . .

Her eyes wandered back to the recipe book. She had better get going on these cookies. Marcia and Melvin were coming back from the park any minute now, and there would be a scene if Melvin's snack wasn't ready and waiting.

She went back to the chocolate. Twelve ounces, or eighteen . . . ?

*   *   *

Bernard was in a bad mood. Snooky had told them all about Freda's untimely death over lunch. Bernard had looked fiercer and fiercer until, with a muffled roar, he had stood up and left the room.

Snooky and Maya gazed pensively at each other.

"I don't know," she said. "Don't look at me."

"He's been so weird for so long now. Have you considered psychotherapy?"

"Bernard is a deeply caring person. These murders are disturbing to him."

"Oh, please, Maya. The only person Bernard has ever cared about is you."

"That's how it should be," she said smugly.

In his study, Bernard switched on the desk lamp, fished around for his Magic Marker and took out his little notebook. In it he guiltily sketched a picture of a sheep with glasses, just to show that in spite of this new and interesting problem, Mrs. Woolly was never far from his thoughts. Then he sat quietly for a while, his mind clicking away in its neat, organized fashion. He was frustrated. The list of possible suspects was shrinking at an alarming rate. Bernard doodled angrily in his notebook. That Simms woman was stupid. She must have seen something, remembered something, and instead of going to the police she had gone straight to the murderer. She had not suspected how dangerous it was. Perhaps she thought that person, whoever it was, was her friend . . .

Or perhaps she had not thought the killer was capable of more violence—was capable of strangling her. Bernard shook his head. Someone who had killed once would always kill again in order to protect their secret.

Bernard looked thoughtfully out the window. Freda Simms had made a mistake, and she had died for it. Another person, too—perhaps more than one—could pay with his or her life. Bernard closed his eyes, trying to imagine himself in the murderer's place. Frightened, now—frightened of discovery, and wary, but satisfied nonetheless. The circle of friends was shrinking rapidly, but so far the police didn't have a clue as to the identity of the murderer. Whoever it was must be very pleased with themselves . . .

Bernard shook his head and sighed. He jotted down some notes. Much as he hated the idea, perhaps it was time for some more definite action on his part. . . .

Mr. Hal was thoroughly enjoying himself.

"Found her myself," he repeated with grisly relish. "Over there. Next to the bookcase. Terrible, isn't it? Just terrible!"

He did not look as if he thought it were terrible at all. Finding his employer's dead body was clearly the most exciting thing that had happened in Harold Shrimpton's life since the Super Bowl.

Detective Voelker sighed to himself. It was going to be impossible to get any lucid story out of the man.

"Face was all blue," Mr. Hal was saying for the fiftieth time. "Terrible-looking. Made me feel faint all over. I was coming in to get my paycheck—I always get paid at the end of the month—and I rang the bell and called her name, but there wasn't no answer. Well, Mrs. Simms always said to me, she says, 'Mr. Hal'—that's what my clients call me, you know, 'Mr. Hal'—'Mr. Hal,' she says, 'you just come inside any time you want, get yourself something cool to drink from the kitchen, just walk inside as if the place were yours.' "

Voelker doubted very much whether Freda Simms had ever said anything remotely resembling that. She had not struck him as the overly generous type.

"Just as if the place were yours, that's what she said," Mr. Hal was continuing with relish. "So today she didn't answer. I walk right in—I do that all the time—and look around and go into the kitchen and say, 'Mrs. Simms?' sort of quiet, you know, in case she's having a nap or something. But there's nobody there, so I help myself to a little bite from the fridge"— Detective Voelker indulged himself at this point with a tight smile and the thought that, had Freda Simms not been beyond the reach of human emotion, she would have been furious to know that Mr. Hal was eating her food—"and then I wander into the living room, saying 'Mrs. Simms? Mrs. Simms?' all the while, and there's no answer. And *then* I see her!"

Mr. Hal clapped his hands to his head for dramatic effect.

"There she is, lying with her face all blue on the rug next to the bookcase! Damned if I didn't have to steady myself, I felt so faint!"

Voelker wondered if steadying himself had involved taking some of Freda's whiskey.

"Yes, Mr. Shrimpton. Very interesting. Let's go over the facts again, shall we? You arrived here—when?"

"Around one o'clock. I always come here at one o'clock, three days a week, Tuesday, Friday and Sunday."

"You work on Sunday?"

"Sure." Mr. Hal looked superior. "I work seven days a week, mister, I don't know about you. I work here Tuesday, Friday and Sunday, and I work over at the Comptons' place Monday, Wednesday and Saturday, and on Thursday I work at the Prices'. I don't mind. It's pleasant work, gardening. Outdoor work. That's what I like. I couldn't stand an office job, if you know what I mean."

Voelker was not interested in the reasons behind Harold Shrimpton's career choice. He frowned and looked through his notes.

"I liked her garden," Mr. Hal said suddenly and unexpectedly. "Beautiful hedges. I trimmed them myself. Unicorns and things, you know. Whatever came to mind. I guess the place'll be sold now," he said wistfully. "Too bad."

"Yes," said Voelker. Connors had questioned the guy, and now he had gone over everything with him twice. He figured he had heard all Mr. Hal had to say on the subject.

It was fairly straightforward. The gardener had knocked on the door, gone into the house, gone into the kitchen, then wandered into the living room, where he had found the body. At that point, whether he needed "steadying" with some whiskey or not, he had acted promptly and efficiently. He had staggered over to the nearest phone and called the police.

The murder was straightforward, too. Strangulation with a narrow rope. Of course there'd be the coroner's report, but there was no doubt about what had happened. The rope had been taken, but the marks were still there.

"Anyone could have done it," Connors said, materializing at his side. "Man or woman. It wouldn't take much strength."

Yes, thought Voelker. From his brief acquaintance with Freda Simms, he would guess that she was drunk when it happened. She would probably not have put up much of a struggle.

His men were checking for fingerprints now. Voelker chewed his lip. They would have to check on her whereabouts last night. Where she had been, who she had been with. Perhaps she had picked up someone at a bar and he had killed her?

Voelker didn't think so. No, he didn't think so at all. The body, according to the medical examiner, showed no signs of sexual abuse.

Robbery?

Nothing had been taken from the house. Freda had had one hundred fifty-three dollars in her wallet, which was still lying on the sofa, untouched. She had an expensive stereo, priceless rugs and works of art. Nothing had been disturbed.

Whoever it was had been very careful, thought Voelker. The doorknob had been wiped clean. It had gleamed in the afternoon sun, faintly mocking them, as Voelker and his men had approached the house. The only fingerprints on it had been Shrimpton's. In all probability the murderer had touched nothing, disturbed nothing, left no traces. He or she had taken nothing except Freda's life.

The whole thing was so damned straightforward, except for the identity of the murderer, which to Voelker's tired and angry brain was as elusive as ever. He looked at Mr. Hal, who was waxing eloquent on the subject of hedge clipping to a bored Detective Connors. Voelker said:

"Excuse me, Mr. Shrimpton. One more thing before you go. How long have you been working here for Mrs. Simms?"

"About a year. Little less than a year. Beautiful garden out there, gentlemen. Just beautiful."

Voelker nodded tiredly. "He can go," he said to Connors.

"Yes, sir."

The man had nothing to do with it, except in his role as Discoverer of the Body, thought Voelker. He rubbed his forehead and said, "Get the car. I'm going over to have a talk with the Sloanes."

"It's not fair."

"What's not fair, Miss Sloane?"

"What happened to Freda." Isabel was looking very tired this afternoon. She had dressed without her usual care in a pair of old jeans and an oversized workshirt. Connors had come by and interviewed her before, breaking the news to her, but Voelker had wanted to talk to her himself. It was obvious that she had been crying.

"It's not fair," she repeated dully. "She was a good person—a good person."

"Murder usually isn't fair," Voelker said. He looked at her curiously. "I didn't realize that you and Mrs. Simms were—so close, Miss Sloane."

Isabel played restlessly with the corner of her shirt.

"We weren't. It's not that, exactly. It's—it's like Laura all over again. Laura and Freda—" Tears welled up in her eyes. "It's so *horrible!*"

"Yes," said Voelker. "Well. I have a few questions to ask you, Miss Sloane, and then you can go. Where were you last night between midnight and two A.M.?" Those hours, according to the invariably reliable medical examiner, were when the strangulation had taken place.

"Asleep," said Isabel.

"Were you here in the house yesterday afternoon?"

"No. I went for a drive in the country."

"I see. Alone?"

"No. With my friend, Snooky Randolph."

"And what time did you get back?"

Isabel hesitated. He could have sworn she blushed. "I don't know. I'm not sure. Around—oh—around eight-thirty or nine, I guess."

"And what time did you go to sleep?"

"Oh, by eleven or so. Richard and I watched television for a while, brought my father up a snack and went to bed—yes—around eleven."

"Miss Sloane, how long would you say it would take to walk to Mrs. Simms's house from here?"

Isabel considered this. "About twenty minutes."

"And to drive?"

"Around five."

Voelker nodded. "How sick is your father *really*, Miss Sloane?"

Isabel looked surprised. "My father hasn't been out of his bedroom since he came home from the hospital, Detective Voelker."

"But he's not actually sick anymore, is he? He's perfectly capable of going downstairs, getting in the car or walking over to Mrs. Simms's house while everyone else was asleep?"

"Yes, he is. And so are my brother and I, which is what you're really thinking, isn't it?"

Voelker shrugged slightly. He was not in the habit of sharing his innermost thoughts with anyone. "Thank you, Miss Sloane. Will you please send in your brother?"

Richard was sullen and evasive. Yes, he had been at home last night. Yes, *all* night. Yes, he had watched television with Isabel. No, he didn't go out for any reason. What were they suggesting? He didn't know anything about it. Could he go now?

What time had he gone to sleep? Around eleven-thirty. Yes, eleven-thirty. He had been keeping late hours recently and he was tired.

Voelker mounted the steps to Walter Sloane's bedroom to find him in a state of near apoplexy. His son and daughter were being harassed by the police. Worse yet, his dinner was late! No, he hadn't been out of the house. He hadn't even been out of his bedroom. No, damn you, he didn't know anything.

"But I'll tell you one thing," Sloane said. "My kids aren't murderers! You're sniffing down the wrong trail, Mr. Know-it-all Policeman! You've got it wrong—all wrong!"

Voelker, fleeing from the room, was inclined to agree with him.

*   *   *

When he went downstairs it was to find Isabel Sloane and her friend What's-his-name Randolph in a somewhat compromising position on the couch. Isabel's head was on her friend's shoulder, his arms were around her and she was crying vociferously.

When Voelker came into the room, Isabel sat up and patted her hair, but the young man's arm stayed over her shoulders.

"Mr. Randolph," Voelker said, "I'd like to ask you some questions."

The young fool was looking ridiculously infatuated, he thought irritably. He looked as if he could barely tear his gaze from the girl's face in order to answer questions concerning a homicide investigation.

His story backed up Isabel's in every detail. Yes, he had dropped her off here last night. She had gone into the house around nine o'clock. It was June and the days were long so they had stayed, ummm, talking in the car for a while.

This was, from his delivery, so obviously a lie that Voelker felt even more irritated.

He had gotten home around nine-fifteen and had been there, at his sister's, all night. He knew nothing about Mrs. Simms's death until Isabel called him an hour or so ago.

Young fool, Voelker thought peevishly. Wonder if they're in it together. He was at both of those parties too. Maybe he wants a rich wife . . .

He asked Isabel whether she knew where Freda had been the night before.

Isabel had no idea. She didn't keep tabs on Freda, you know. No, she didn't know any places where Freda liked to hang out. That was her own private business. Although she imagined Freda was probably out somewhere, if it was Saturday night. Freda was very popular with men.

And that's that, thought Voelker. Nobody knows anything and Freda Simms could have been out anywhere.

As he left the room he felt, rather than saw, the two young people collapsing on each other again.

*   *   *

Heather Crandall, contrary to Voelker's expectations, had quite a lot to say about Freda's death. None of it was interesting or relevant, but she delivered it with a great deal of vigor.

"Something has to be done about this investigation," she said severely. "These murders can't be allowed to continue. It's a disgrace to the neighborhood, a positive disgrace. Soon I won't be able to let my children walk to school. As a mother and as a concerned citizen, Officer, I must protest."

Voelker regarded her wearily. "Yes, ma'am."

"I warned Freda about her lifestyle," fumed Heather. "I warned her. I said, Freda, my dear, all this hanging around in bars and picking up strange men is going to be your death someday. Yes, it is. I warned her. I told her so."

"Yes, ma'am. I'm sure you did."

Unexpectedly, Heather warmed up to him. "I'm sorry, Officer. I'm sure you think I'm way out of line, talking to you like this. It's just that I feel I've gotten to know you during this terrible time. You look tired. Would you like some tea?"

Detective Voelker didn't think so. Neither did Detective Connors, who had stayed to supervise the investigation at the Simms house and had joined him at the Crandalls'.

"Do you know any of the bars or nightclubs that Mrs. Simms frequented?"

No, said Heather. She looked surprised and a little disapproving. Of course not. How would she know?

"You feel sure that Mrs. Simms was killed by a man she had picked up somewhere?"

Heather looked even more surprised.

"Of course," she said. "What other explanation could there be? Naturally it was some stranger she met and took home. She *would* invite people home, in spite of all the times I told her . . . well." It was dangerous, of course, she went on, but Freda would persist in her habits. See where it got her in the end.

"You don't think the murderer could have been— someone she knew?"

Heather looked shocked. Someone she knew? How could that be? No, no, it was a stranger. Somebody she met at one of those bars she went to. There were a lot of dangerous people out there, she said primly. Psychotics. They looked all right, then they turned on you. Surely the detective would know about that?

"There's a word for it," she said. "Psychopaths. People with no social conscience. They kill just for the pleasure of it. It gives them a feeling of power—of control. And sometimes they look absolutely all right. So, you see, there's no way of *knowing*."

Yes, said Detective Voelker, looking at her rather oddly. Yes.

Just before he took his leave, he asked whom she had told about Mrs. Simms's death.

"Well, Harry, of course. He's not here right now, he's at the university. He's in the lab all week long, even on Sundays, although I do try to discourage him. And of course I called Ruth Abrams as soon as I heard."

Yes, said Voelker. Of course.

Ruth Abrams met Detective Voelker at the door with a plateful of overbaked chocolate chip cookies. That was about all he got out of her. Yes, Heather had told her on the phone; yes, yes, terrible, wasn't it? Other than that she knew nothing. Her husband said the same.

Both couples had told him that they were sound asleep at eleven o'clock the night before. They seemed surprised that he would even ask. Of course, thought Voelker, one of them could have gotten up, gone downstairs and taken the car over to Freda's without waking the other one. Or maybe one couple was in it together. This was a confounded business. He said so later to Connors, with a great deal of heat.

"One of them is lying," he said. "One of them is lying. But damned if I know which one it is."

Connors said he thought it was the girl. The Sloane girl. No reason to believe her story. That Simms woman could have seen her put something in her father's drink.

"She stands to inherit a lot if her father dies," Connors

pointed out. "She and her brother. She couldn't have the Simms woman getting in the way."

"If that's the case, why hasn't she done her father in already?"

"Biding her time. That's what she's doing. Just biding her time. Waiting until all this blows over."

Voelker shook his head. Perhaps . . . but he was inclined to think not. Walter Sloane had been safe in his own home, waited on and protected by his two children. Surely if they had wanted to murder him they could have done so by now.

"This is a confounded business," he said out loud, and Connors agreed.

Bernard looked doubtfully at the piece of paper in front of him. On it, in his neat green handwriting, was printed

Pty dd—y hve t in 1 pce—cnfsng!
Nlss—nthr nmly?

Bernard contemplated this in silence. Finally he leaned back in his chair and called, "Maya?"

Snooky appeared at the study door. "Maya's out, Bernard."

"Oh. Okay. Can you make head or tail of this?"

Snooky took the paper and glibly read:

"Pitty did—why have tea in one piece—confissing! Endless—nither numly?"

"Thank you."

"These the notes for your book?"

"No."

"What are they, then?"

"Just some notes I made to myself."

"That your special shorthand system?"

"Yes."

"Well, it works great, Bernard. I can see that."

Bernard looked at the piece of paper again. "I knew what I meant at the time."

Snooky concentrated hard.

"Pretty dead," he said at last in triumph. "Why heave it in one piece—confessing! Unless—in there nimbly?"

"Thank you, Snooky."

"Anytime."

Snooky was in the living room an hour later, deep in a book, when Maya entered with a determined look on her face. "Snooky, I have to talk to you—now."

"Fine." He put down his book. His sister eyed it dubiously. "What's that?" she said.

Snooky turned it over. It was called *UFO's: Our Friends from Outer Space*.

"I found it on the shelf in Bernard's study. It's interesting."

"Bernard? That's impossible. Bernard would never read that."

"Why? He doesn't believe in UFO's?"

"It's not that. For Bernard, the universe is crowded enough as it is. The thought of other planets being inhabited makes his flesh creep."

"Well, it was on his shelf, Maya. Either there's a part of him you don't know about, or maybe visitors from outer space put it there."

"I have to talk to you," Maya repeated.

"You're doing okay so far."

"I've been thinking about you and your friend Isabel."

"What a coincidence. So have I."

"Honestly, I think she's bad for you, Snooky. I don't think you're in love with her. Of course you're not. Love is something completely different."

"Okay."

"I think this is just another one of your silly hare-brained affairs, which last a few days or weeks and always seem to end with you coming to visit us. Am I making myself clear?"

"Perfectly."

"There have been three murders around that girl and for all we know, she could have committed them. Yes, she could have. Don't wince and look away. Something extremely peculiar is going on. And I'm worried about you.

You're young and stupid. I know you won't drop her right away because you're convinced you're in love, but I wish you'd be more careful. She could be just using you to back up her story or alibi or whatever it is. There's something very cold and self-centered about her and neither Bernard nor I like it. I know you don't see it, but it's there."

"Okay."

"Anyway, please be careful. I don't know what you're getting yourself mixed up with."

"I will, Maya. I'll be careful."

"You're not really listening to me, are you?" asked Maya in despair.

"No."

"But you're going to be angry at me later anyway, aren't you?"

"Probably." He picked up the book. "But hey, maybe the aliens will land and we'll all have something else to think about by then. Hey, My—did you know that there are places in Peru where their ships go by every night?"

In the Sloane house, another brother and sister were talking.

Richard said, "You know I didn't have anything to do with—with what happened to Freda, don't you?"

"Oh, Richard. Don't be ridiculous. Of course you didn't."

There was the sound of a little bell from upstairs. Isabel had given her father a bell to ring when he needed something.

"Oh, *hell*," said Isabel expressively, and went upstairs to the sickroom.

"Yes, Daddy?"

"I want some milk," her father snarled. "Some *hot* milk, with chocolate in it and some of those marshmallows— the little ones."

Isabel looked at him, puzzled. "But, Daddy—you've never had cocoa in your life."

"Well, I want it now. And bring it quick, will you?"

Honestly, thought Isabel, going back downstairs, he could be *pregnant* for all the demands he makes. He's just enjoying himself, like the big baby he is. She went into the kitchen and pulled the cocoa mix out of the cupboard.

She found a half-empty bag of tiny marshmallows, sticky and encrusted with goo, and opened it gingerly. "Ugh," she said, lifting some out. Well, they would have to do. She knew her father well enough to know that plain cocoa without marshmallows, when he was in this mood, would definitely not be acceptable.

She carried the mug back upstairs and entered his room. He was propped up against the pillows, reading.

"What's that, Daddy?"

"Essays. Montaigne," her father grunted. "Thought I might as well keep up with my reading for the next time I have to talk to that great bore, Harry Crandall. Thought I'd be prepared."

Isabel paused by his dressing table. When would that be, she wondered. When would her father feel safe again in the company of his friends?

"Leave it there and turn off the overhead light as you go," her father said in a kindlier tone. "And Isabel—"

"Yes, Dad?"

"Thanks," he said unexpectedly, glancing up from his book. "You're a good girl, you know that?"

"Yes, Daddy. I know."

As she went out, she turned to switch off the light and flashed him a look of hatred and scorn!

It was the next day, Monday, and Detective Voelker was sitting in his office surrounded by lab reports. He perused them worriedly.

Someone besides Freda Simms and the gardener had left fingerprints in the living room. These prints were not on file; nor did they match the fingerprints of any of the Sloanes or their friends.

The coroner's report merely confirmed what Voelker had suspected. Freda Simms had been drinking heavily on Saturday night.

Voelker scowled at the fingerprints. Who was this? Probably someone who had picked up Freda in a bar—or vice versa—and brought her home. This mystery man could have been the one who strangled her. He could have been . . . but somehow Voelker didn't think so. No, he didn't think so. He was fairly sure these prints had nothing to do with the murder.

He had his men out combing the local bars and restaurants looking for anyone who had seen Freda Simms last Saturday night. And the man she might have been with. Voelker would like to have a long talk with him. Of course she could have met him anywhere. And it would take time . . . lots of time.

He shook his head and continued reading the reports.

"Of course we're going to the funeral," Heather said. "Wait a minute, Ruth. Harry, you can't wear that—no, go change—I *mean* it, Harry—that tie is atrocious. This is a solemn occasion." Into the phone she said, "Well, naturally we're going. I mean, poor *Freda*."

"Yes," concurred Ruth doubtfully. "I suppose—I suppose we'll be going, too. I guess we'd better start getting ready. Sam doesn't want to go and neither do I—you see, Heather, I mean, it's not as if we knew her all that well—but I guess we really should . . ."

"Of course you should. We'll see you there, then."

"Yes—" said Ruth's hesitant voice as Heather hung up with a sharp *click*. Heather turned to survey her husband.

"No, *no*, Harry," she said in exasperation. "No, not that tie either. Are you out of your mind? Flamingos at a funeral?"

Snooky drained his cup of coffee and stood up.

"Well, I'd better get dressed. The funeral's in an hour. I'm meeting Isabel there beforehand."

"Be careful," Maya said.

"I will. Bernard, can I borrow your jacket? You know, the dark one?"

"No."

"Why not?"

"Because I'm going to wear it."

"Wear it? Wear it where?"

"To the funeral."

Snooky and Maya gaped at him.

"But sweetheart," Maya said, "you don't have to go to this funeral. You didn't even know the woman."

"I know," said Bernard, rising ponderously to his feet. "I want to go."

"Why, for God's sake?"

"I want to meet all of Snooky's little friends," said Bernard.

The funeral was a solemn affair, although no one cried. Funerals at which no one cries are sadder occasions than funerals at which everyone cries. The reception, hosted by an elderly aunt of Freda's who had turned up at the last minute and claimed all her money, was terribly grim. It was made even grimmer by the presence of Bernard, who sat in a corner and stared balefully at all the guests. To everyone's surprise, Isabel and Richard appeared with their father firmly sandwiched between them; Isabel had been determined that he should come and pay his respects to the dead. There were plenty of people at the reception; Freda was one of those essentially lonely people who gather others around them like a magnet. There were more men than women. One of Freda's friends-and-acquaintances, a gifted puppeteer, enacted a puppet mime show over the coffin. Another, a poet, brought red roses. Yet another spent his time explaining to Ruth Abrams, who was trying very hard not to listen, what a very *special* person Freda had been.

"Yes, yes," said Ruth irritably, wondering what she had done to attract this—this *person* and what she could do to extricate herself. "Yes . . . of course . . . oh yes, she was, she was."

Freda's aunt, who at the age of seventy-six was now suddenly and spectacularly wealthy, gave Freda a nice going-away party.

"For that's how I think of it," she fluted, her voice carrying across the room, "as just a little going-away party. Of course Freda's just on the Other Side—you know that, don't you?—the Other Side . . ."

She intended to devote the rest of her life and all of Freda's personal fortune to research in parapsychology.

"Just a going-away party," she trilled delightedly. "I'm sure she's here somewhere, enjoying herself . . ."

Bernard, upon hearing this, wished that she were. Perhaps then he could ask her to point out her murderer.

For of course her murderer was here. His eyes scanned the room. Maya, Snooky, Isabel, Richard, Walter Sloane. Heather and Harry Crandall—there. He recognized Heather from the visit to his house. Ruth and Sam Abrams—over there. Snooky had pointed them out to him at the funeral. Ruth was looking at a young man who was monopolizing her as if she wished he were in the coffin instead of Freda.

Bernard heaved himself slowly to his feet and crossed the room.

"Maya," he said. "Introduce me to these people."

Maya looked startled but obediently did so. She had just met most of them herself.

"Heather and Harry, this is my husband Bernard . . . Sam, Ruth, my husband Bernard . . . you know Isabel already, of course . . . this is her father, Walter Sloane and her brother Richard. . . ."

Bernard remarked to Heather Crandall that he was tremendously sorry about the incident with Linus and the ears.

Heather looked charmed and said it was all right. Children were so fanciful, weren't they? They lived in a world of their own, and believed nearly everything that was told them. She told Bernard that he must have had very strange karma with Linus in order to frighten him so much at first meeting.

Ruth Abrams was obviously grateful to be rescued from her persecutor and talked to Bernard for quite a while about cats. Ruth loved cats. Why, they had owned a cat as far back as she could remember. . . .

The funeral seemed to have dampened Harry Crandall's garrulousness. He spoke briefly to Bernard about *The Tibetan Book of the Dead*, but his heart was not in it. He stood to one side, looking pale and saying little. Walter and Sam were standing together awkwardly. Bernard moved over to them and began to talk. . . .

By the time the reception was over, Bernard had spoken to everyone in the ill-fated circle around the Sloanes. In the car on the way home he was silent, as usual. Maya regarded him nervously.

"It's so *unlike* you, Bernard. I don't understand it."

Bernard smiled.

A week later Sam Abrams was rooting about in his basement workshop. He kept all sorts of things down there. There was a sewing machine (broken), a workbench, three old rusty filing cabinets, one kid's chest of drawers from when Marcia was young, the cat box, piles of old wire and rope, and a set of tools. He had promised Ruth that he would clean it up sometime, and he kept promising, but somehow it never happened. He liked it the way it was. The only problem was, it was so messy that most of the time he didn't know where things were. Right now he was looking for a Phillips screwdriver, a small one. He thought he had put it over there on the bench, but it wasn't there

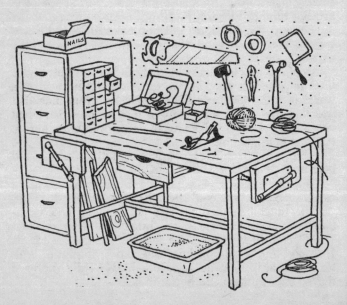

now, and unless the cat had knocked it off he wasn't sure where it could be.

He would have to get this place organized, he thought, arms crossed, looking around him. Ruth was right, it really was a mess. He had gotten everything nicely organized at work—all the file cabinets in order for once, everything filed away neatly—now that the employees could work and concentrate without cringing before Walter's bellowing voice. Yes, everything was running smoothly there, for once. He felt good about that.

But this basement was another problem. Now where *was* that screwdriver? He supposed he could use a nail file or something like that if he had to, but it wouldn't be nearly as good. . . .

It was somewhere between the piles of old newspaper and the discarded cardboard boxes that he realized that the pest killer was missing. It was a new kind, very expensive, and he had bought just a little bag of it to try this summer on the lawn. The plants *would* get red spider mites and mealybug, and nothing seemed to help, but this product advertised, "Pests gone in five days." Five days! He'd believe it when he saw it. In his experience mealybug could run through an entire plant population, inside *and* outside.

He looked around doubtfully. Wasn't it here that . . . no, well, maybe not. He thought he had put the bag of insecticide on this shelf here, next to the old brown bottle of dried-up ointment, but maybe not. Or perhaps the cat had gotten to it and it was somewhere on the floor, being batted around like a toy mouse.

He cursed and surged forward again in search of the Phillips screwdriver. He really *would* have to clean up the basement one of these days!

9

Jim Voelker sat at his desk, hunched over in frustration. He was looking through his files on the Sloane case.

Voelker had a methodical turn of mind. His notes were carefully kept and neatly organized. He had a list of the people involved and their various interconnections. He had doctors' reports, medical examiner's reports, fingerprints and background data. He had transcripts of interviews, names, addresses, dates and photographs. All of which had gotten him nowhere.

He sat back with a curse. Damn it, he thought. There were only a few suspects in this case. It should be obvious. Surely the murderer would have overplayed his or her hand by now. . . .

But they hadn't. They remained as safe as they were in the very beginning, and somewhere, in a nice suburban home, one that he had visited, somebody was laughing at him even now.

The thought made him furious. He stood up and kicked the wastepaper basket. It fell over and rolled away. The other detectives in the room glanced at each other but said nothing. They knew better than to interfere with Voelker when he was in one of his Moods. That was how they referred to it around the department, one of his Moods with a capital M. Voelker was a likable guy but he had a temper when he got going.

Voelker grimaced to himself. He knew he had a bad

temper but he usually managed to hold it in. His friends usually told him that he bottled it up *too* much, rather than the opposite.

Bottled it up . . .

That got him thinking . . .

Who was it among these people who bottled things up, perhaps for a long time, in silence?

Who was it who held things inside until one day they couldn't hold it in any longer?

Who was the *nicest* person in this group of ill-fated friends?

He sat down and went back through his files again. . . .

Meanwhile, Bernard and Snooky were having another one of their face-offs in the study.

"So you're sure," Bernard was saying, "you're absolutely *sure* you didn't see anyone tamper with Sloane's glass at that first party?"

"I'm sure."

"It must have been very cleverly done. Think, Snooky. Didn't you see *anything*?"

Snooky closed his eyes for a moment, then shrugged. "You have to understand, Bernard. I didn't know anyone was about to be poisoned. I'm not clairvoyant. As I recall, I spent most of the evening worrying that the hors d'oeuvres were going to run out."

"Yet that woman must have seen something."

"Freda?"

"Yes."

Bernard stared out of the window. Snooky, frustrated, picked up a rubber band and began to twang it vigorously. "I've thought about it over and over again," he said, "and I haven't come up with *anything*. Everyone was acting normally. They all seemed to be having a good time. Those parties were just like a hundred others I've been to, except that somebody died. I'm telling you, Bernard, to me it doesn't add up. It just doesn't make any *sense*."

"Oh!"

"What? What is it?"

Bernard remained silent.

"What? What did I say? What is it? What are you thinking about?"

Bernard shook his head slowly.

"Nothing. Thank you, Snooky. It's just something—something I should have realized a long time ago. . . ."

Jonathan, Marcia and Melvin had finally departed, driving off in a cloud of dust with plenty of shrieked "good-byes," and Ruth felt extremely relieved. She told Heather so.

"I'm *extremely* relieved."

"Yes. It was a drag to have the kids around, wasn't it?"

Ruth thought about this. It wasn't exactly a drag, it was . . . it was hard to put her feelings into words. . . .

"No. I don't know. I guess so. I guess it was," she said unhappily. "It's not that I don't love seeing them, of course I do. It's just so—so *difficult*."

"You're such a nice person, Ruthie," Heather said, sitting down at the kitchen table with a cup of murky brown liquid. "Some twig tea?"

"Yes, thanks."

"You should have thrown them all out days ago."

"Oh, Heather. I can't. I can't do that. They're my *children*."

Heather could do that, Ruth thought, almost enviously. She looked at her friend—so tall, so slender, so capable—she knew how to handle her family. She had Harry twisted around her little finger, and the boys did whatever she said.

Ruth had never been that way. Her kids had run rampant over her from the time they learned to walk and talk. She was just a big mushy pushover, that's what she was. Even Sam bossed her around sometimes.

Thinking of Sam reminded her. She said, "You know, Heather, Sam found the strangest thing the other day."

"What's that?"

"Well, he was in the basement, in his workshop," Ruth said, her face going all pink, "and even though he was looking for something else he realized—well, he realized all at once that the insect killer was gone. You know. We bought this new kind to try this summer—our lawn is such a mess, we're really embarrassed in front of the neighbors—

just a little box of it, and now we can't find it. He called me down and we both looked for it, but it simply isn't there. Unless, of course, the cat could have gotten hold of it. . . ."

"That's odd," Heather said. She put down her cup and looked gravely at her friend. "That's very odd. Insecticide, you say?"

Ruth nodded hopelessly. "And it *worries* me, you know, because of all these terrible things that keep happening . . . we wondered whether it had something to do with it."

"I think the police were looking for a certain kind of insecticide. Yes, I'm sure they were."

"Oh!" said Ruth nervously. "Maybe—maybe I should go tell them?"

"On the other hand, maybe your cat has it."

"He does get into everything," Ruth said vaguely. "The cat, I mean. You can't trust him anywhere. I don't know. I could go to the police, Heather, and it could turn out to be nothing, nothing at all—I'd be so *embarrassed*. What if they turned the basement upside down, and it turned out the cat had taken it somewhere and hidden it to play with?"

"Was it in a box?"

"A bag. A little bag, about this big." She gestured. "Perfect for the cat to get his claws into."

"Maybe the cat buried it somewhere."

Ruth looked doubtful. "Ye-e-es," she said. "I suppose so."

"Ruth, who's been in your basement in the past few months?"

"Oh, my goodness, I don't *know*. Really! I don't know if I could *say*—"

"Think, Ruth. It might be important."

Ruth thought. She thought very hard. It was a novel experience for her, and not unenjoyable. She drank her twig tea and thought it over while Heather drummed her fingers softly on the table.

"This is fun. It's sort of like sleuthing, isn't it?"

"Ruth, this isn't fun at all. It's serious. Now, who's been down in Sam's workshop?"

"Well—well, of course, the kids have been in and out. And Melvin's down there whenever Sam will let him."

"The kids don't count. Think, Ruth. Who among our circle of friends?"

Ruth thought. She cogitated deeply. A worried frown appeared on her face. Her forehead wrinkled even more than usual. Finally she looked up with a sigh.

"Nobody," she said.

"That's impossible."

"It's not. I mean—nobody! No one's been down in that basement except for Sam. Why would they, after all? There's nothing down there but junk. Well, not *junk*, exactly. Sam's projects."

"Who's been over at your house, then? Who knew about the new insecticide you had?"

"Oh, goodness, Heather, *everybody* knew! Sam told everybody about it. He was all excited, you see—it was supposed to get rid of mealybugs in five days—we've had such problems with—"

"He didn't tell me," Heather said.

Ruth looked at her doubtfully. "Are you sure? Really? I could have sworn that at the tennis party—"

"I'm sure. I never heard about it."

"I thought everyone knew," Ruth said miserably. "Who thought it was important, anyway? I can't remember things like that."

"Listen, Ruth. You have to go to the police about this. Yes, you do," Heather said firmly, seeing the look of dismay on her friend's face.

"But, Heather, *nobody* could have taken it—it's probably just somewhere on the floor, you know, where the cat's been playing with it . . ." Her voice died away as she saw Heather's expression. "You don't believe that, do you?"

"No, I don't. Neither do you. You're not as dim as you make yourself out to be, are you, Ruth darling? You have to go to the police."

"I can't," Ruth wailed. "They found my fingerprints on that glass. I'm a *suspect*!"

"All the more reason for you to go to them with what you know."

"Murder and mayhem," Ruth said tearfully, staring into her teacup. "'Murder and mayhem.'"

"You don't want to end up like Freda, now do you? Go to the police."

"Oh, all *right*," Ruth said miserably.

Heather was that way: when she said something, you did it. She had her family twisted around her little finger; and, Ruth thought resentfully, now *she* was being bullied by her too!

Voelker's men went over the basement inch by inch. The packet of insecticide was gone. Sam Abrams stood by unhelpfully, saying things like:

"Please don't move that—that's my new project—oh no, you can't move *that*, that's fragile—this is an old TV I'm going to fix one of these days—be careful with those cabinets, the drawers are about to break—I'll fix that too, I've been planning to for a long time now— it's so difficult to find the time, isn't it?—oh, please, be *careful*—!"

Voelker did not say a word until the search was finished. Then he went upstairs and said to Connors, "Not much help."

Connors nodded. "It's gone, all right."

"It was the right kind, too. I checked it out with the medical examiner. Who's been down in this basement?"

On this point, Ruth was equally as unhelpful as her husband had been. She didn't know who could have been in the basement. Nobody, really. Or anyone. I mean, how could you tell? They had had their friends over in the past few months, any number of times. Anyone could have slipped downstairs for a minute. There was that tennis party they had given about a month ago . . . of course *they* didn't have a tennis court, but their neighbors owned one and let them use it sometimes . . . it was really very kind of them, wasn't it? No, none of their visitors had asked to see the basement. Why would they? That would be odd, wouldn't it?

She asked the last question sharply, her dull brown eyes going back and forth between the two policemen. That would certainly be odd, wouldn't it?

Yes, yes, it would be odd, said Voelker. Whom had the Abramses had over since they bought the insecticide?

Ruth got terribly muddled. She thought that they had asked Heather and Harry over—for bridge, you know, they enjoyed the game so much, and when Walter wasn't around there was none of that awful yelling. Then after that Laura and Freda had come over for coffee one afternoon, and the three of them had had such a good talk . . . wait a minute. Her brow creased. Was that before or after Sam had gotten the insecticide? Goodness, it was all so *difficult*. . . .

Finally, after much rumination and hesitation, the answer boiled down to one simple fact.

All of the Abramses' friends had been over either before or after the arrival of the insecticide.

It was impossible to pin down exactly when they had visited. Pondering this, Ruth grew confused and her answers became even more muddled and self-contradictory.

"Perhaps we had the Crandalls over before," she would say with disarming frankness, then later add, "or perhaps it was afterward, and Isabel and Richard dropped by with Laura before that. Yes, yes, it's all so *confusing*, isn't it?"

During these visits, any or all of the guests apparently had unlimited opportunity to slip downstairs and seize the packet. The basement stairs were in the laundry room off the kitchen. All one had to do was excuse oneself for a glass of water, then go quickly downstairs and back up again. The basement door was always left open.

"Well, of course it is." Ruth hastened to explain. "Sam goes up and down all the time, and the cat sleeps down there. I don't know exactly *where* he sleeps, poor thing. Probably on a pile of Sam's old machinery. We made a bed for him out of blankets, but he never seems to use it. Isn't that just like a cat?"

Voelker gave her a long hard stare. Was she really this dim-witted, or was she hiding something?

In the end, when his questions began to repeat themselves with no noticeable improvement in the replies, he gave up.

"Thank you, Mrs. Abrams," he said grimly. "We'll be in touch."

"Oh, I'm sure you will, Officer," Ruth said almost gaily. "I'm sure you will."

She closed the door behind him and leaned against it with a heartfelt sigh of relief.

"Isabel and I are going out to dinner," said Snooky. "Don't cook for me tonight, okay, Maya?"

Maya was proofreading one of her magazine articles. "Okay," she said. "That'll cut our food bills in half."

"And I have more news for Bernard."

Bernard sipped his coffee thoughtfully as Snooky told him about the missing insecticide. When he was done, Bernard said:

"I see."

"Does that fit into your theories, Bernard?"

"Maybe."

Snooky waited, but that seemed to be all Bernard had to say. Snooky turned to Maya. "Has he always been this garrulous, or is it just me?"

"It's just you."

"Oh. Okay."

Maya adjusted her reading glasses. "Bernard doesn't go around blabbing about everything to everyone. You wouldn't understand."

"I don't go around blabbing, either," said Snooky, offended.

"To Bernard, murder isn't a laughing matter. He has a highly developed moral sense. You wouldn't understand."

"I don't get it. Why do we talk about him as if he's not here? Have aliens stolen his brain?"

"By the way, what time will you be home tonight?"

Snooky regarded her in amazement. "What are you, my mother?"

"Just wondering."

"I'll be home by eight-thirty. I'll get into my jammies and we can have milk and cookies, okay?"

"Okay." Maya went back to her article. Bernard was staring off into space.

"I wonder—" he murmured.

He became aware of their expectant gazes. He looked down at his coffee cup and said with dignity,

"Yes. I *wonder* if there's any coffee left?"

Having secured the car through an exercise in quick talking, Snooky took Isabel out for a meal at an extremely expensive French restaurant.

They sat at a candlelit table in a dark corner and held hands. Isabel was looking very beautiful. Her shining blonde hair was pulled back from her face and fastened with a jeweled clip. She wore gold earrings and deep red lipstick.

"Have some more fish," Snooky was saying.

"Thanks." She looked at him approvingly. The candlelight suffused his pale face with a reddish glow. He wore a jacket and tie and looked very well in it.

She told him so.

"Thanks," said Snooky. "Have some more fish."

"I've had enough."

"This is the most delicious fish I've ever had in my life. I feel I've never truly lived until this moment."

"You eat more than anybody I ever knew. I'd forgotten about that."

They talked about many things: about college; about their experiences since then, Snooky roving all over, Isabel staying at home; about their siblings. They did not discuss anything remotely connected with murder. It was a fine evening and there was no need to spoil it.

"I wish I had traveled the way you have," she said with a sigh. "Lately—I don't know—for a while now I've been thinking how much fun it must be to go places. I've never been anywhere."

"Oh, you have to travel. See the world. It's wonderful. There's nothing like it."

"You're really lucky, you know that?"

"It's not luck. It's a matter of choice. I decided a long time ago that's what I wanted to do. And remember, it makes me a moving target for William."

Later she said, "That jacket looks very good on you, Snooky. You should dress up more often."

"What, this little thing?" he said carelessly. "It's okay. It was the best Bernard had."

"Oh. I see. And the tie is Bernard's, too?"

"Yes. Can you believe he only owns two ties, and they're identical?"

"Why not? Apparently you don't own any."

"No, but if I did, they'd be nicer than this."

The waiter materialized at Snooky's elbow and paused expectantly.

"Ah, yes. Dessert. What would you like, Isabel?"

"Oh, nothing. Just some coffee."

"Coffee for the lady," said Snooky in his lordliest manner, "and for me, the largest dessert you have."

"*Pardon?*"

"You heard me. Coffee for the lady, and for me, your biggest dessert."

"One of our *pâtisseries, peut-être?* Or a cake, a slice of *gâteau au chocolat* . . . ?"

"It doesn't matter. Just so long as it's extremely large."

The waiter dematerialized. Isabel lit a cigarette.

"You shouldn't smoke, you know," said Snooky. "Terrible habit."

"It relaxes me."

"Poisons your lungs."

"Please, Snooky. You sound like Heather."

Isabel's coffee arrived, and with it, the largest slice of chocolate cake, piled high with almonds and chocolate shavings, that she had ever seen. Snooky looked pleased.

"*Formidable*," he said. "*Précisément ce que je voulais.*"

The waiter fluttered happily, like a giant butterfly. "*Merci, monsieur.*"

On the way home (the waiter had accepted Snooky's extravagant tip with a gratified smirk), the subject of Richard came up.

"I'm worried about him," Isabel said. She looked out the window of the car and the streetlights played over her face. "You know I'd do anything for him. We've always been close. But recently he's started—I don't know—drawing away from me. He won't talk, won't answer when I ask him why. He goes out at all hours—sometimes I don't even know he's out or where he is—and I don't know who his friends are."

"You're not his mother, Isabel."

"In a way I feel like I am. Our mother died so long ago . . . and I'm so much older than him. I feel responsible."

"When I was a teenager and started getting away from Maya, she was so happy she cried."

"Well, I'm not. He's just—he's been acting so strangely."

When they got to Isabel's house they walked into the middle of a scene.

Richard and his father were facing each other across the living room. Both were plainly furious. Richard was pale, and his father's eyes were nearly bulging out of his head.

"You lazy good-for-nothing!" he was shouting as they came in the door. "Don't do your homework, run around all day and night with God knows who—your lazy friends—can't take care of me when I need you—"

"You don't need me here! You're such a big baby! You can go into the kitchen and get your dinner yourself! I'm tired of waiting on you hand and foot!"

"You left me all alone here!" shouted his father. His voice had an uneven, ragged quality to it: the sound of fear. "All alone! Anyone could have come in that door! *Anyone!*"

"Oh, Dad, you're so paranoid. Nobody's after you," Richard said in disgust. "I wanted to go out with my friends for a while. Just out to get something to eat—"

"And left me all alone!"

"Oh, Dad, *honestly*—!"

Both heads turned as Isabel and Snooky came into the room. Both mouths snapped shut.

"What's going on here? What's wrong?" asked Isabel angrily.

"Nothing."

"Nothing."

The three of them looked at Snooky.

"Yes. I was just leaving," he said.

Isabel saw him to the door and gave him a warm kiss good night.

"Thanks for a lovely evening," she whispered. "I'm sorry it had to end like this. I left Richard in charge, and of course they had to go and have one of their fights."

"It's okay. Will I see you soon?"

"Of course."

On his way home Snooky tried to listen to the radio, but his thoughts were crowding in on him, demanding attention. He had seen or heard three things tonight that worried him, revolving round and round in his mind.

One was the raw sound of fear in Sloane's voice as he said to his son, *You left me all alone* . . .

The second was the look of anger and hatred on Richard's face tonight . . .

The third was Isabel, very composed, very beautiful, saying about Richard, *You know I'd do anything for him* . . .

Anything for him . . .

Anything . . . !

10

Snooky came into Bernard's study the next day and sat down, his long legs sprawled out in front of him. He glanced at the desk, which was littered with papers, paper clips tortured into unrecognizable shapes, rubber bands, pencilless erasers and eraserless pencils, pens of all different colors and sizes and a small silver-framed picture of Maya. He said, "Hi. Are you working?"

"Yes," Bernard said sullenly.

"Am I bothering you?"

"Yes."

"Do you mind if I talk to you?"

"Yes."

"That's right," Snooky said. "Refuse to hold out your hand to a person who's drowning. Stand on the shore and look the other way. Who am I, anyway? No one. Just your wife's favorite brother."

This had the desired effect. Bernard looked surlier than ever, doodled furiously on a scrap of paper, closed his notebook, then moved his chair an inch or two toward Snooky and waited.

"Thanks so much. Here is my problem. It concerns Isabel."

At the sound of her name Bernard gave a short ugly laugh.

"I suppose that it hasn't escaped you that she's a suspect for murder," said Snooky.

"It doesn't surprise me, if that's what you mean. Most of your girlfriends have had criminal records."

"I'm worried about her, Bernard. I really am. The way she talks about her father and her brother, it's—it's not right. There's something weird about it. She's very close to her brother, and—oh, I don't know. She's ten years older than Richard and she talks like she's his mother. It's strange. And yet her own life is a total mess. She can't make plans from one day to the next."

"Thank you for sharing all this with me."

"I'm in love with her, but I don't know how she feels about me. She's always been that way . . . hard to understand. I never know what she's thinking. The woman's a complete mystery."

He paused.

"I was hoping you'd give me some man-to-man advice. I feel we don't have enough of these talks, Bernard—manly talks, you know. Man-to-man stuff. Maya wouldn't understand. I felt I could come to you."

"Yes," said Bernard. "Thank you. I think you should dump her. I hope we can have a talk like this again sometime soon."

Later Snooky wandered into the kitchen, where he found Maya with her head in the fridge. She was rooting frantically for some mushrooms.

"I *know* they're in here somewhere," she said in a frustrated tone. "I just know—ah!—no, that's not them—how about down here—oh my God, what's that?—*ugh*. I'll let Bernard get rid of *that*, I don't want to go near it. And what's over here?—God, that's disgusting—now where were those stupid—"

"Do you know what you're like, Maya? You're just like one of those pigs they keep for rooting out truffles. You really are. You could make money that way."

Maya found the mushrooms and as punishment Snooky was set to chopping them. As he worked he said disconsolately, "My?"

"Mmmmm?"

"Do you think there's any chance Isabel could have committed those crimes?"

"You mean, do I think your girlfriend is a cold-blooded murderer?" Maya was busy trying to unscrew the top of a jar of tomato sauce.

"That's right."

"With your taste in women, Snooky, I'd say it's perfectly possible."

Detective Voelker was unhappy. He was more than unhappy; he was miserable. They had searched three houses top to bottom and there was no trace of the missing insecticide.

Two corpses, one near-corpse and no evidence at all! Nothing! He chewed on a fingernail and felt ill-tempered; decidedly ill-tempered. Connors and the others were staying out of his way. Damn this investigation!

They had run up against a wall. They had done everything right, questioned everyone concerned, followed every step, yet this case was not unraveling. Rather the opposite. Before his eyes he seemed to see the various threads of it winding tighter and tighter together. False clues; false leads; false hopes. Damn it!

He cast an evil glance at his subordinate when Connors came up to talk to him.

"Don't say anything," he snapped. "Don't talk to the others, don't say a word. And above all, don't tell West the state this investigation is in."

Connors said respectfully, but with a not unreasonable amount of glee (he had had his eye on Voelker's position for a while),

"Yes, *sir*!"

"Oh, good," said Maya. "He's grunting."

"He's what?"

"He's grunting."

Snooky listened. From inside Bernard's study came a series of happy grunts.

"That's Bernard?"

"Yes."

"You're kidding."

"He always grunts like that when his work is going well. It's a good sign."

"I worry about you, you know that, Maya?"

Inside the study, Bernard was sitting in the dark. His brain was working furiously. Snooky, in one of their recent conversations, had inadvertently said something interesting . . . something that had given him an idea . . . an idea that made all his other thoughts settle finally and irrevocably into place.

He switched on the light, took out his notebook and wrote,

$$\$\$\$\$ \text{ ?}$$

Then:

JEALOUSY

POWER

and

TH CNTR SHFTS

"The center shifts," he said, and grunted cheerfully.

He pondered for a while, then wrote out a small equation. It said simply:

$$2 + 1 \neq 3$$

He tapped his pen on the paper. Yes . . .

He leaned back in his chair and shifted his feet. The dog let out a sleepy snarl.

Two plus one does not equal three . . .

"*Yes*," said Bernard.

"Sam?"

"Yes, Ruth?"

Sam Abrams turned to find his wife clutching a piece of pale blue paper.

"Sam, where is Kuala Lumpur?"

"Kuala Lumpur?" He thought for a minute. "I think it's in Malaysia. Yes, I'm sure it is. Why?"

Ruth's lips trembled and he saw to his shock that she was having difficulty holding back tears.

"Because that's where Marcia is right now."

"*What?*" He tore the paper out of her hand. It was a letter in his daughter's characteristic slanted script.

"Dear Mom and Dad," it said. "Please believe me, I know what I'm doing. I've met a wonderful man and Melvin and I are going to Kuala Lumpur with him. He says the mountains there are wonderful and there are places where you can go and see the stars . . ."

Sam scanned it rapidly.

". . . so really don't worry, it's going to be terrific. Melvin is all excited about it, too." And with Marcia's typical second sight, she had scrawled at the end, ". . . I'm sure right now Mom is crying and Dad is furious, but by the time you get this we'll be out of the country, so believe me, there's nothing you can do. Don't alert the authorities, okay? Call you as soon as we get back—love, Marcia and Melvin."

Typically, there was no mention of when that might be. Marcia had also neglected to mention the name of the wonderful man who was accompanying them.

"Kuala Lumpur," Ruth said tearfully, and threw herself on the couch.

*   *   *

That night Sam and Ruth were at dinner, both of them pecking dispiritedly at Ruth's latest culinary disappointment, when the phone rang. Sam rose thankfully and went into the kitchen to answer it.

"Hello?"

"Sam? This is Walter."

"Walter? How—how are you?"

"Getting better. Recovering. How's the business?"

"Fine. It's fine. Couldn't be better."

"Does everyone there miss me?"

At Sam's silence Walter Sloane gave a short bark of laughter.

"No, I'm sure they don't. Sam, I'm calling to tell you that I'll be back soon. A couple of days at the most. The doctor checked me out and says I'm fine."

"Oh, good . . . good." Sam hoped he sounded more enthusiastic than he felt. "So we can expect you back by the end of the week?"

"That's right."

"But, Walter—do you really think that's wise?"

"Why not, Sam?" Walter sounded amused. "None of my friends work where I do—none except for you, of course—and you wouldn't try to kill me, would you?"

He laughed at Sam's discomfiture.

They talked for a little while longer, then Sam hung up the phone and came back into the dining room. Ruth looked up.

"What is it?"

He told her, and they sat silently around the table, lost in their thoughts. Finally Ruth speared the chicken leg on her plate and banged it up and down. She said angrily,

"It's not fair—that's all—it's not *fair!*"

Meanwhile, Heather had her own hands full.

Linus had been sent home from school in a considerable state of disarray after being beaten up by one of his classmates: a girl. He did not seem particularly mortified by this, although Heather knew that once Harry heard about it there would be strong words on the subject. Linus's explanation was brief and to the point.

"She likes me."

Heather sat down on the couch and stared at her son.

"If she likes you," she asked reasonably, "why would she beat you up?"

Linus shrugged. "She wanted to play with me and Timmie, and I told her we didn't want to play with her, so she beat me up."

He seemed resigned to this.

"Everybody saw it," he said proudly.

Heather reflected that she would never understand the workings of the five-year-old mind.

"I hope you hit her," she said, lowering her voice in case Harry came in.

"I tried to, Mommy, but she's too big. Her arms are longer than mine."

"I'm going to have a little talk with her mother," Heather said grimly. She knew the girl in question. Her name was Angela Elwood and she was taller than all her classmates, something that (Heather thought vengefully) no doubt contributed to her social maladjustment.

She cleaned up Linus and changed his clothes and he went off happily to play for the rest of the afternoon. To his mind, the crucial point about the whole affair was that he got to come home early from school.

Heather studied his blond head lovingly as he bent over his toys. He was such an *odd* child—so quiet, so self-contained—surely there was something wrong about that? She remembered herself as a youngster—tantrums, petty rebellions—her life had been one long vale of tears from age three to age twenty-one. And here she had spawned these three serene, well-adjusted youngsters. How was it possible? What were they hiding? Surely Linus must be *angry* . . .

But he didn't seem angry. He seemed perfectly content as he played with his toys. He lay on his stomach and ran a plastic truck back and forth on the carpet.

"*Vroom . . . vrooooommmmmmm . . .*"

The telephone rang and Heather, shaking off dark thoughts, went to pick it up.

Ruth's voice was loud and anxious and she seemed upset. Of course, that was Ruth; always another crisis.

"What?" Heather said, her mind on her troubles with Linus. "What did you say?"

What was it that Ruth was talking about? Something about koala bears—Australia—

"Kuala Lumpur? You're kidding! How long?"

Ruth didn't know. Ruth was miserable. Sam was upstairs banging his head against the wall.

And there was the news about Walter finally returning to work . . .

Heather was very interested in this.

"I've been planning to go over there and visit him for a while now," she said. "Want to come along?"

Ruth sounded shocked.

"Oh, no, no, no, you can't, Heather! He's not seeing *anyone*. Why, he won't even let you in."

Heather's gaze wandered through the door to where Linus lay on the floor.

"Oh, yes he will. I've been meaning to go by and say hello and drop off some cookies. It's ridiculous, the way none of us dares to visit him. And he's coming out in a few days anyway, isn't he?"

"Well—" Ruth sounded doubtful.

"You don't have to come, Ruth. Think it over. Listen, I have to go now. Talk to you later."

As she hung up Heather thought,

That new recipe . . . those peanut butter oatmeal cookies would be perfect . . . I'll mix some up tonight. . . .

Bernard was squinting worriedly at his notebook, which lay open in front of him on the desk.

He had an interesting idea. There was no proof, of course—nothing definite. The person he was thinking of was too clever for that. No, there was no proof and never would be. Not unless . . .

Bernard felt a troubling moment of self-doubt. Who was he, after all, to think he might have solved the puzzle of these crimes? No one—nobody at all!—just the writer of the Mrs. Woolly books. Why, he didn't even *know* the people involved.

But even as he thought that, he realized what a tremendous advantage not knowing them was in this case. No one else could see the truth. To enter that circle of friends was to feel the center shift. . . .

He knew that his customary reserve and distrust of his own species had helped him think clearly. He trusted no one and believed no one. It was his most marked trait and, in this case, his greatest advantage.

He drummed his fingers on the desktop. At his feet Misty got up, tail thumping, expecting dinner.

Bernard pondered for a while. Misty, measuring his attitude with a practiced eye, lay down again with a long whistle of regret.

Bernard was worried; even alarmed. The more he thought everything over, the more worried he became. There was a certain ruthlessness about these crimes that bothered him. The murderer had struck three times and would not hesitate to strike again. . . .

Eventually he did what he always did when upset or worried. He went to find Maya.

He found her in the living room, sitting on the window seat with Snooky. Bernard looked lovingly at his wife. The moonlight streamed into the room and lit up her angular face, making her look very beautiful. Seeing the two of them, so similar in appearance, so close together, Bernard felt a curious pang of love and jealousy. Maya and Snooky were like twins, in spite of the five-year age difference; they were so close and had shared things together that he could never share.

"Bernard," she greeted him. "Snooky just bet me a dollar that he can complete the *New York Times* crossword puzzle in fifteen minutes. Want to join in?"

"The Sunday *Times*," added Snooky. "The Sunday *Times*, mind you."

"No, thanks," said Bernard. He sat down heavily in his favorite overstuffed armchair. "Maya?"

"Yes?"

"The time has come to act. We must act quickly."

They gazed at him in mild astonishment.

"Quickly," repeated Bernard. "Time is short."

"Has he always talked this way?" said Snooky. "Like an oracle?"

"Snooky, I want you to call that policeman. The one that keeps coming here and interviewing you every three minutes."

"Gladly, Bernard."

"Plus I need your advice about something—a very delicate matter. . . ."

Isabel opened her front door to find Heather and Linus Crandall on the doorstep. Heather was balancing a plate in one hand and grasping Linus firmly with the other.

"Hello," she said cheerfully. "I've just come by to drop off some cookies. Where's your father?"

"In his study. But Heather, you can't, he'll—"

"Nonsense. He won't refuse to see me. Come on, Linus."

The two of them brushed past Isabel. Heather marched determinedly down the hall and flung open the door.

"Hello, Walter."

He glanced up from his desk in surprise.

"I've brought you some cookies," said Heather, still grimly cheerful, "and Linus wants to say hello."

She pushed Linus forward.

"Hi, Uncle Wally."

"I'll leave him here with you for a while. I'm going to visit with Isabel. These cookies will be in the kitchen if you want more, Walter. Here. Take a couple now."

She put a handful down on his desk.

"Can I have some?" asked Linus eagerly.

Heather looked disapproving. "No, you can't, sweetheart. You've already had too many at home."

"I didn't have *any* at home!"

"Yes, you did, Linus. You're going to spoil your appetite for dinner. So long, Walter. Nice seeing you. Remember to have those cookies."

She was gone before Walter had time to say a word.

"They'll keep each other company," Heather said, bustling back into the kitchen. "Can I trouble you for some herbal tea, dear?"

Isabel, filling the kettle with water, noticed how sharply the other woman was watching her. *She's intelligent,*

Isabel thought with a twinge of surprise . . . *she knows what she's doing, barging in here like this* . . . .

She had always written Heather off as a bit of a crank, but it came to her all at once that, for all her various affectations, Heather knew precisely the kind of effect she was making on people. Other people were taken in, but she wasn't. . . .

"Have a cookie," Heather was saying, holding one out toward her. "They're delicious. Linus had three before coming over here. Peanut butter and oatmeal. Very high in protein and fiber. Here, have one."

"Thanks," said Isabel. She bit into the cookie. "Why, it's great. Richard will love these."

"Boys," said Heather with a sigh. "Don't I know it! I can't bake enough for my three. Nothing stays in the house for long. I have to apologize, by the way, dear. I know your father doesn't want to see me, and I'm sure you have better things to do with your time. But I heard he's going back to work in a few days, and I did want to come over here and break the ice."

"Well, now, that's really nice," Isabel said cautiously. "It's certainly been bothering me, the way Daddy's been avoiding everyone. I think it's great if he gets back into circulation."

"Ruth Abrams would have come with me, except—well, you know Ruth. She felt she wouldn't have been welcome. Here, have another cookie."

"Oh, that's silly. You'll have to tell her to come by sometime."

"These tragedies," Heather said, spreading her hands expressively. "It's so hard to know what to do or say afterward, isn't it? Plus I feel what happened to your father is partly my fault—oh yes, I do—since it happened in my house. Tell me, how is Richard handling everything?"

Her gaze on Isabel seemed uncomfortably sharp. . . .

"He's fine. Just fine."

"Oh, that's good, because sometimes shocks like that can upset boys his age so much that they never let it out. Charlie is like that. He won't talk about what's bothering him. I sit with him and try to get him to talk, but he won't. He's very good at getting around me. That's something that kids get good at as they grow up—wouldn't you agree?—getting around their parents, I mean."

"Yes, well. I guess so." *Has she heard about Richard's running around and fighting with Dad?* Isabel was wondering. *Gossipy bitch! What else does she know?*

"Ruth tells me all kinds of things about her kids," Heather was saying. "Terrible problems she has, really terrible. Now her daughter has just left for Malaysia on the spur of the moment. Can you imagine? And of course she told me all about the missing insecticide. Whoever used it *would* steal it from Ruth, because she's so fuddle-headed that it's unlikely she'd ever notice. And Sam's workshop is really a mess. Did they search your house, too?"

The question was sharp.

"Of course," Isabel said without thinking.

Heather nodded as if satisfied. "They searched ours from top to bottom. Linus thought it was all a big game. He followed the policemen around and asked them questions. What are you doing? What are you looking for? He wanted to look, too. That's the way children are—so curious. Of course they didn't find anything in any of our houses. I could have told them that from the start. Whoever stole that stuff must have gotten rid of it as soon as possible. Don't you think so?"

"Yes . . . well . . . I guess so. I don't really know."

"That's what *I* would have done," Heather said firmly.

Richard entered the room and Isabel greeted him with relief. "Hi, Richard. Heather brought us some delicious cookies. Want one?"

"Mmmm," said Richard after biting into one. "Great!" He scooped up three more and pocketed them, leaving the room.

Heather and Isabel burst into laughter.

"Boys!" said Heather.

In the study, peace and quiet reigned. Linus had settled down with a pad of paper and a crayon and was busily drawing what looked like a herd of elephants. Walter was at his desk, working.

Occasionally they exchanged a comment or two, nothing more. Walter was absorbed in his work and Linus was content to be drawing. Between the two of them was an instinctive rapport. Linus studied his elephants with a critical eye and, crossing them out, began to draw stars, a skyful of stars.

Out in the hallway the door bell rang and they could hear Isabel answering it.

"Oh, *hello*," she said. "Come on in . . . Heather's here too, of course . . ."

Her voice drifted away into silence. The breeze from the open window ruffled Walter's iron-gray hair.

Linus happily colored in the spaces between the stars to look like the night sky. Finally he rolled over with a little sigh. He lay on his back, hands crossed on his stomach, watching Walter.

Finally he said, "Uncle Wally?"

"Mmmhmmm?"

"What was that stuff you drank after everybody left Mommy's party?"

"What?"

"That stuff. That stuff. You put it in a glass and went to the punchbowl and put some punch in and drank it."

Walter Sloane looked up.

"I didn't put anything in any glass."

"Oh, yes you did. I saw you. I was under the table. I like being under the table," Linus said in a meditative voice. "You can see people and they can't see you. It's fun."

There was a long silence.

"You must be mistaken, Linus."

Linus looked puzzled. He rolled over onto his stomach.

"I don't think so. Don't you remember, Uncle Wally? You weren't feeling good. Mommy and Daddy ran out of the room, and it was just you and me. Except you didn't know I was there."

There was another pause.

"Well, yes, now that you mention it, I think I do remember what you're talking about. It was when I was alone in the room, wasn't it, after I had come in from outside?"

"Uh-huh."

"Well, well. It's nothing to worry about, Linus. It was just some medicine I always carry with me. I was feeling sick, so I took it and it helped me."

"Did it?"

"Yes."

"That's good."

Linus, losing interest, picked up his crayon and began to draw goldfish swimming in a pond. The goldfish were so large that two of them filled up the whole page. He chewed his lip, disappointed, and started over again.

The man at the desk spoke.

"You haven't told anyone else about this, have you, Linus?"

"Unh-unh."

"Okay. That's good. I wouldn't want anyone to worry, you see."

Suddenly a rather flustered voice spoke from the study door.

"Oh!" it said nervously.

Walter Sloane spun around in his chair. "Who's there? Who is it?"

Ruth Abrams edged sideways into the room, like a crab.

"It's me. Just me. Ruth. How . . . how are you, Walter?"

"Ruth? What are you doing here?"

"Linus," she said falteringly, "Linus, your mother wants you. It's time for you to go. She's waiting for you outside."

"Oh. Okay." Linus gathered up his crayons. "Bye, Uncle Wally."

Walter Sloane gave him a grim smile. "Good-bye, Linus."

"Bye, Aunt Ruth."

Ruth shut the door firmly behind him and gave Walter Sloane a nervous little glance. "Boys! *So* imaginative, aren't they? Such—such tales they love to tell." Her face was all pink and her gray curls bobbed helplessly. "Boys . . . yes . . . oh, yes . . . such little tales they love to tell."

She came over and sat down in front of the desk. "Why, I remember my Jonathan at that age. *Such* an imagination! Why, the things he used to tell me . . . you would never have believed it."

"Yes. Well. Listen, Ruth. I've got a lot of work to do before I go back to the office next week—"

Ruth gave a strange little gasp. "Of course, I happen to know that what Linus told you is true—isn't it?"

There was a silence.

"I don't know what you heard while you were eavesdropping at the door, but I can assure you, it was nothing. Just a little game between Linus and me. As you said, lots of boys play games like that. It was nothing."

"Oh, yes, yes, yes, of course it wasn't. Yes, Walter, I quite understand. Of course it wasn't. Of course no one would believe what Linus had to say, would they?—no, no—very convenient for you, isn't it? But it's different with me, you see, Walter. It's different. Because, you see, *I know you did it*."

She smiled at him brightly.

"Yes. You killed Laura and Freda—oh, poor Freda, just because she happened to see something at one of those awful, awful parties. I had a bad feeling before the first party. Yes, I did. I said, 'Sam, we shouldn't go. Something's wrong. Something terrible is going to happen.' But of course we had to go. You and Sam have been business partners for so long—well, it wouldn't have looked *right* if we didn't."

"I don't know what you're talking about."

"Oh, no, no, no, of *course* you don't, Walter, and you don't have to if you don't want to, it's all right with me. But let me tell you my side of it. You see, I've been thinking things over for quite a long time now." She put her head to one side like a little bird and her face went all pink again. "I know that thinking about things isn't my strong point," she said humbly. "But ever since that bag of insecticide was missing from our basement, I've been thinking things over in my own way, you know. And even though I told that policeman that I couldn't remember if anyone had been down in the basement before it disappeared —of course I couldn't at the time, you see, I was so upset and flustered and I just *hate* anything having to do with the police, don't you?—well, afterward I was thinking it over and it seemed to me that that wasn't quite true. Because I suddenly remembered that somebody had been down in the basement. At the tennis party. And it was you, Walter."

She looked at him expectantly.

"You see, everyone else had been over our house any number of times—Laura and Freda and Isabel and of course Heather and Harry, and Richard never comes over at all if he can help it, and naturally it's hard to keep things straight when you're not sure exactly when it was that people were over or when that little bag disappeared. Oh, it's very hard indeed. But I was thinking it all over in my own way, slowly, but if I may say so myself, *carefully*, and it suddenly came clear to me."

She paused and looked at him again.

"You see, everyone else had been over any number of times—*but you hadn't*, had you, Walter? You never come over our house. The only time I could remember your being there was at the tennis party we had, a few weeks before Laura's party. There was something about that party you didn't know, Walter—something I didn't even remember until just a few days ago. You see, I came back to the kitchen at one point—I had to get the watermelon out of the fridge and also we had run completely out of ice, I don't know why that always happens to us—and I was in the kitchen and I saw you, Walter."

She nodded emphatically.

"*I saw you coming up the basement stairs.*"

She nodded again.

"I meant to ask you at the time what you were doing down there, but you went out the back door and I was so worried about the ice—I mean, there's no way of making ice in a hurry, is there, and everyone's drinks were warm—that I forgot all about it. It didn't seem important, you see. But then I started thinking about it and I realized that you must be the one behind all these dreadful murders. Because you were in our basement that day, and you took the poison. And then you used it to kill Laura. And later I suppose you poisoned yourself at Heather's party, just to throw everyone off the track. Then you killed Freda to keep her from talking. Really, when you think about it, it's all very clear, isn't it?"

There was a pause.

At last Sloane said, "Why are you lying like this, Ruth? Have you gone completely crazy?"

"Now, now, Walter. Don't start in. I'm not lying. You know that perfectly well. Now listen to me. I came here today for a good reason—yes, a very good reason. Heather said she was coming over, and Sam told me you were going back to work soon, and I thought about it and realized that this is the perfect time to ask you for a few little favors."

She sounded very smug.

"*What?*"

"A few little favors, Walter," she said calmly. "I want money—not enough to break you, just enough to help Sam and me get by. And I want you to promise that you won't go back to work—not tomorrow, not next week, not *ever*. I want Sam to take over the business. You see, Walter, I hate to say this, but I think he deserves it a lot more than you do."

She looked at him placidly.

"You're out of your mind."

"No, no. I don't think so. I think you're going to do just what I say. Because if you don't, I'll go to the police. I know them by now, you see, I have a personal connection."

"It'll be your word against mine."

"Yes, it will, won't it? My word—and Linus's—against yours."

"Your word and Linus's!" He laughed. "You're crazy! Who in the world is going to listen to a five-year-old—and a half-wit like you?"

"Well, I never! Half-wit! I *never*! Why, if Sam could hear you say that—!"

He leaned forward menacingly.

"You have a damned good reason for wanting to incriminate me. I'd tell the police you want Sam to take over my position. Nobody—*nobody*—would believe you, Ruth."

Ruth shook her head at him pityingly.

"You still don't understand, do you, Walter? They don't *have* to believe me. All they have to do is begin—*just begin*—to suspect you. Don't you see? The only reason you've been safe this long is that *no one has considered you as a possibility.* Once I tell my story—and what I heard Linus say—they'll investigate you all over again. They'll haul you in and ask you all kinds of questions—embarrassing questions. You know what I mean, Walter. And they'll find the proof. Of course they will. You know that. That's why you tried so hard to protect yourself, isn't it? Once they suspect you, it'll just be a matter of time."

She stood, picked up her frayed handbag and moved toward the door.

"But if you would rather I went and told them *now*—"

Walter Sloane spoke heavily.

"Wait!"

He reached down and opened a drawer. Taking out his checkbook, he said, "How much?"

"Fifty thousand dollars," she said promptly. "To start with. I've been planning to buy some new lawn furniture, and it's *so* expensive, don't you think? And there are some renovations we've been wanting to do for such a very long time on the house . . ."

She took the check and said:

"Very wise of you, Walter. Very wise."

"Get out."

"Wait a minute. Wait a minute. I'm not done with you yet." She sat down again. "I want your promise that you won't go back to work."

"No!"

"Promise me, Walter. You won't go back to work, will you? You'll give up your position and let Sam take over, now won't you?"

"All right. All *right!* Now *get out!*"

She sat looking at him calmly, the check clutched in her hand.

Sloane's nerves gave way.

"What is it?" he roared. "What is it, damn you? *What more do you want?*"

She rose to her feet and leaned over the desk. There was something very beautiful in her face as she spoke.

"Justice," she said.

Walter Sloane stared unbelievingly as the door opened and the policemen filed in. . . .

Ruth handed the check to Detective Voelker and whirled on Walter Sloane as he got up from his chair. She slapped him smartly across the face and shrilled:

"And *that's* for calling me a half-wit!"

11

"Eat your dinner," said Maya.

Snooky pushed his plate away. "I'm not hungry."

"Eat your dinner. Have some cabbage, at least. It's good for you."

"I don't want cabbage," Snooky said irritably. "I hate cabbage. I've always hated cabbage. You know that. Why are you torturing me? Why can't I go talk to Bernard?"

He looked longingly at the closed study door.

"Bernard's busy right now. Anyway, he explained everything to you yesterday. Weren't you listening?"

"Yes, My, but I want the *details*."

"Cabbage before details," she said firmly, and with a sigh Snooky picked up his fork.

Inside the study, Detective Voelker was having trouble drawing out Bernard, whose instinctive hatred of his own kind had returned in force once he considered the case closed. He sat at his massive desk and stared palely at the policeman. Misty mumbled, teasing a rubber bone at his feet.

"But what," Voelker was saying patiently, "made you guess that Walter Sloane was the murderer?"

Bernard didn't know. It was a number of things. Things that didn't fit in. Things that didn't make sense.

"For a while there I admit I thought your brother-in-law might have done it," said Voelker. "His girlfriend is going to be a very wealthy woman now."

Bernard greeted this with incredulity.

"Snooky? *Snooky?* I assure you, Detective, my brother-in-law could not put together a successful plan to murder a rodent. If Snooky wanted to murder someone he'd just come at them with a battle-ax."

"Yes. I see. What exactly then were these things that didn't make sense to you, Mr. Woodruff?"

Bernard glanced through his notes nervously. He drew out one page that had the word

ANMLYS

written in large green letters at the top.

"Anomalies," he explained. "I was struck by how many there were. First of all, Sloane didn't die. It seemed strange to me at the time. His wife was poisoned, and she died; Freda Simms was strangled, and she died; Sloane was poisoned—but he didn't die. Well, why not?"

"It might have been a mistake in the dose."

"Yes. But the doctor said the dose was large enough to kill."

"Yes—that's true."

"Then there were some other strange things, things that didn't fit in. For instance, the second party—the one that Heather Crandall gave. That didn't make sense to me at all. Why would Walter Sloane go? He was supposed to be a suspicious, paranoid individual. This was the same crowd that had allegedly poisoned his wife. Yet he accepted the invitation. It didn't make sense. And even if he did attend, why would he let Heather Crandall touch his glass, take it away to fill it up, and so on? Wouldn't he be more careful than that? No one ever told me that Sloane was a stupid man, but that was a stupid thing to do. It felt all wrong to me, somehow."

"Yes. I see."

"Of course, he had to go to that party. He needed someplace—a public place with all his friends present—to stage his own poisoning." Bernard looked thoughtfully out the window. "It was clever—very clever—*very* risky. The man took an awful chance. He knew he'd be the main suspect when his wife was killed. So what does he do? He arranges to poison himself, very realistically. He faked his symptoms in front of the Crandalls. When they left the room to get help, he picked up the nearest glass, dumped in a carefully premeasured dose of insecticide, went to the punch bowl, ladled in some punch and drank it down. Then he went back and knocked over the lamp as if he were in convulsions. He had it all planned. That way, he'd get to the hospital in plenty of time to receive the antidote, but a blood test would show that there was a toxic amount of poison in his system."

"And the glass he used had been used during the party by Mrs. Abrams, so her fingerprints were all over it," said Voelker. "We looked in the wrong direction that time—at her instead of at him."

"Which is what he figured would happen, so he felt safe. The self-poisoning worked very well. It shifted suspicion off of him and onto an unknown murderer. He then proceeded to build up the existence of this nameless murderer, this enemy, implying that his friends were all potential killers while at the same time protesting their innocence. Once his basic premise had been accepted—that his wife's murder was either an accident or part of a series that included him—he felt fairly safe."

"Yes."

"I believed it, too," said Bernard. "For a long time my suspicions were focused on Heather Crandall. Why did she give that party, for instance? She had that family connection to the Sloanes. There might have been a financial motive there. But one day Snooky and I were talking and he said to me, 'It just doesn't add up,' and I thought, that's right, it *doesn't*—it's not a series—there's an anomaly right in the middle of it." Bernard glanced down at his notes, which read:

$$2 + 1 \neq 3$$

"Two murders and one murder *attempt*. I realized they didn't belong together—they didn't add up. After all, what actually happened? Laura Sloane and Freda Simms died. Freda Simms's death wasn't planned in advance, that much was clear—she had been killed because she knew something. *So the only murder that was planned in advance was Laura Sloane's,* and who had the primary motive for wanting her dead? Her husband, of course."

He sat silently for a while, then said, "Laura Sloane must have been a fascinating person. Wealthy, lively, attractive. But she needed to control everyone around her. Look at Freda Simms—she never forgot her, never forgave her for marrying, never really let go."

"And Sloane hated being controlled."

"Oh, yes. But he couldn't divorce her—she wasn't the forgiving type. She'd leave him without a penny. She had a habit—one I'm sure he detested—of taking drinks out of his hand and finishing them herself. That's how he must have gotten the idea. All he had to do was slip some poison into his glass, pretend to be drunker than he really was, and wait. If it hadn't worked, he could have dumped it somewhere and no one would have suspected."

"That might not have been the first time he tried it There were other parties."

"Yes. True."

"We've found the man who was with Freda Simms the night she died," said Voelker. "We've got a record of the call she placed from the phone booth outside the bar to Sloane's house. The two kids must have been asleep by then—it was after midnight—and Sloane picked up the phone. She was stupid enough, or drunk enough, to threaten him. Her companion says he brought her home about an hour later, barely able to walk, much less defend herself. Sloane must have been waiting outside."

Bernard said slowly:

"A ruthless man."

"Yes. By the way, it was a clever trap, Mr. Woodruff. Was it your idea to get Mrs. Abrams to try to blackmail him?"

"Oh, no. I asked Snooky about it. It was clear she had the best motive, but I wondered whether she could handle it. Snooky thought she could."

"So now all the money goes to the boy and girl. Wonder what they'll do with it? Hundreds of millions, from what I hear."

"It's not much of a way to inherit," said Bernard.

The next day, in Isabel's house, Snooky asked very much the same question.

"All that money. What're you going to do with it?"

"I don't want to discuss the money. I don't want to even think about it."

"But, Isabel—"

"I mean it. Not a word!"

He subsided.

Isabel was wandering around the living room, angrily picking up pillows and throwing them back down on the sofa.

"The money! The money!" she said bitterly. "I never wanted to get it *this way* . . . !"

"I understand."

"You do not."

"I do. Come sit down and calm yourself, my girl."

She flopped down next to him. "I don't want to talk about it. I don't want to talk about anything. I just want to be alone."

"Fine. Shall I leave?"

"No . . . no. Sit here for a while."

Snooky sat there. Isabel leaned her head against his shoulder. He could feel the tension slowly ebbing out of her body. Finally she said in a quieter voice, "I'm going to sell this house. Richard and I can't live here anymore, of course. I'll sell it. Then, well, Richard will be going to college next year. I'll buy a house near him, so I'll have someplace to come home to."

"And then?"

"Then I think I'll travel. I've always wanted to, you know. Freda and Laura used to talk about traveling—how much they loved it . . ." Her voice trailed off.

"That's nice. Go to Malaysia. I hear it's beautiful this time of year."

"I've always wanted to see New Zealand."

"Supposed to be very nice."

"Or Australia."

"Supposed to be great. Can you hear my heart breaking?"

She twisted to look up at him. "Oh, don't be ridiculous, Snooky. We'll still see each other."

"Where? Somewhere in the Far East?"

"Oh, you know. Here and there."

"Here and there," he said heavily. "Yes."

Isabel looked troubled.

"You're such a good person," she said remorsefully. "I never—I never wanted to *hurt* you."

"The words of death," he duly reported to Maya later. "Words of death. 'I never wanted to *hurt* you,' emphasis on the '*hurt*.' Pffftt!! End of a perfectly decent relationship."

"I've never been so happy to hear anything in my entire life."

"She's going to travel, she says. Travel! When she could be with *me*. Do you understand that?"

"You could travel with her."

"She didn't ask me to."

"Well, then that's that, I would say. It's over, Snookers. Get used to it."

"She says she'll see me here and there. Here and there! Do you know what that means, My?"

"Yes," said Maya. "It means 'good-bye.' "

As Snooky left the Sloanes' house, Isabel said bitterly, "Best wishes to your sister and Bernard, okay? Especially Bernard. Without him I wouldn't be a rich woman today, would I?"

At the door Snooky paused and looked back. Isabel was alone in the big room, moving back and forth restlessly, running her hands over everything. She seemed unable to stop moving. Looking at her, he was suddenly reminded of Freda—of her nervous gestures, her luxurious house, her desire to travel. To get away from it all. To run away . . .

He closed the door and left.

"I was wrong," Heather was saying on the phone to Ruth. "Completely wrong. I was sure it was either Isabel or Richard. That was why I wanted to go over there. I asked her all kinds of questions, but she seemed perfectly innocent. And all the time Linus was in the study with—with—"

"Oh, it's too horrible to think about."

"You may have saved his life by going in there when you did, Ruth. Really. You'll never know how grateful we are."

"Oh, please, Heather. Please—please don't. Don't be silly. Anyway, Walter would never have—have done anything to hurt Linus. You know that. Why, he *loved* Linus."

"You know, I think he did."

"Of course he did."

"Still, you were brave, Ruth. Very brave."

"Oh!" said Ruth, pleased. "Oh! Well . . . *somebody* had to do it. That's what Mr. Woodruff said, when he came by with the detective and Snooky. He said that somebody had to do it, and I was the best one, because I had the best motive. Can you imagine? The best motive for *blackmail!*" She giggled. "So I agreed, naturally—not that I've ever done anything like that before—just my high school play, *George Washington Slept Here*, but I had a very *small* part, not a speaking role at all. And Sam didn't want me to do it, we had quite a little disagreement, but in the end he saw it made sense. You see, I *wanted* to do it, for him—for Sam, you know. After all, why should he have to work for a murderer?"

"Yes," said Heather, thinking what a very Ruthlike thing that was to say.

"How is Linus now?"

Heather glanced into the living room. "He's fine, just fine. Nothing seems to disturb that child. I don't understand it. It must be all the foods high in B vitamins I give him. He's stable as a rock. Which is something I've been meaning to tell you, Ruth—"

"How's Harry?" Ruth asked, for once in her life adroitly cutting her off.

"Harry? He says there's no one to argue with now that Walter is gone."

Ruth tried to feel some sympathy toward this point of view and failed.

"And Sam?" asked Heather. "How's he taking everything?"

Ruth felt embarrassed. Sam was in charge of the business now and he was loving every minute of it. Their lifestyle would not change drastically, but at least she no longer had that empty feeling—that terrible envy—inside of her. She could go to the supermarket and not count pennies.

"It's awful, Heather, but he loves it," she said, dropping her voice. "And—I can't help it, either—I feel *happy.*"

"Horrors!" said Heather, smiling.

Maya, Bernard and Snooky sat in a comfortable circle in the living room. There were steaming cups of coffee at their side and each had a different section of the newspaper.

Bernard had the crossword puzzle, Maya had the News of the Week in Review, and Snooky had the television page, which he was reading the way other people read Dostoyevsky.

"Twelve down," announced Bernard. "Smooth-surfaced yarn, seven letters, blank O blank blank T blank blank."

"Worsted," said Snooky.

Bernard looked irritated. "Now how would you know something like that?"

"I just know."

After a pause Bernard said, "Chagall's hometown. Seven letters. Starts with a V."

"Vitebsk."

"Fourteen across. Five letters, blank M O blank blank. Silvery salmon."

"Smolt."

Bernard looked over at his wife in chagrin. "When's he leaving?"

Maya folded the newspaper. "Bernard," she said patiently, "if you're going to ask for help with the crossword, then you can't complain about getting the answers. I've told you: Snooky is good at things like that. It's about the only thing he *is* good at."

"In answer to your question, Bernard," said Snooky, "I'm leaving tomorrow. My bags are packed and ready at the door. I leave, by the way, with a heart dimmed with sadness."

"Just as long as you leave."

"His heart is broken," said Maya cheerfully. "Broken! Based on past experience I give him three days to recover."

Her brother glanced at her. "You think I'm an emotionally shallow person, don't you?"

"Three days," said Maya. "Four, tops."

Snooky shrugged. "There's a good program on this Thursday. Do you think William will let me use his TV, or will it be off-limits?"

Bernard made a faint choking sound. "You're not going to *William's*?"

"Oh, yes I am. Didn't I tell you? Another letter has arrived, protesting my lifestyle, and I've decided to go directly to ground zero and discuss it with William in person. Right now I imagine Emily is in a tizzy, trying to figure out what delicacy to cook for me."

"Emily doesn't cook," Maya informed him. "Neither does William. Neither do their kids. They eat out every night."

"So much the better."

Misty bumped against Bernard's leg, asking for a walk.

"Just a minute," Bernard said absently. "Snooky, one more answer, if you please. My brain isn't working tonight. Six letters, blank blank I blank blank blank. The clue is, 'Oak or sumac, in common.'"

Maya looked at him disapprovingly over her reading glasses.

"Bernard, you should know that," she said. "The answer is *'poison'*!"

Gloria Dank is married and lives in New York City.

THE MYSTERIOUS WORLD OF AGATHA CHRISTIE

Kinsey Millhone is . . .

"The best new private eye."   *—The Detroit News*

"A tough-cookie with a soft center."   *—Newsweek*

"A stand-out specimen of the new female operatives."
—Philadelphia Inquirer

Sue Grafton is . . .

The Shamus and Anthony Award winning creator of Kinsey Millhone and quite simply one of the hottest new mystery writers around.

Bantam is . . .

The proud publisher of Sue Grafton's Kinsey Millhone mysteries: